ORIGINS:
A TERRAMATES NOVEL

LISA LACE

ORIGINS
Copyright © 2016 Toppings Publishing.
All rights reserved.

CONTENTS

CHAPTER 1

SOPHIE

"I'm never getting married, and I'm never going to have children. It goes against everything I believe in, Mother." I rolled my eyes when she turned her back. "I'm making my commitment today."

Why couldn't she get it through her head that I had made up my mind and wasn't going to change it?

"Twenty-six is pretty young to be deciding such a thing, Sophie. Can you have any consistent beliefs before you're thirty?" She pulled our lunch out of the fabricator. It never tasted as good as food cooked the old-fashioned way, but it was a lot faster than working in the kitchen. "I'll be honest with you, honey. You've never been in love, and you don't know what you're talking about. You might change your mind. I don't want your future determined by a ridiculous, idealistic club."

I'm sure she wanted to call Single for Life something else. She'd made it pretty clear she didn't have any respect for my beliefs. She thought it was a cult or something, which irritated me. It was the furthest thing from a cult I could imagine. It was a group of thoughtful people who were taking concrete steps to deal with overpopulation instead of merely talking about it.

If enough people stopped having children, we had a chance of solving the population crisis. The number of humans on Earth was beginning to exceed the limits of the planet. It was my opportunity to show that I was an adult and that I could make mature decisions, like deciding to join Single for Life.

I huffed impatiently. I felt irritated but determined at the same time. For goodness sake, I'd been working for them for over two years now. That should have given her plenty of time to realize no grandchildren were coming out of me.

"Mother, you can't argue with the facts. Earth can't handle any more people. We're on the verge of exhausting its resources. If we don't stop having children, we're going to have to start evacuating Earth. EarthGov is already starting to apply for refugee status on other planets."

"I know, Sophie. But what's the point of saving the world at the cost of ruining your life? If you have no descendants, why do you care about the future of the planet?"

"Sometimes an individual has to make sacrifices for the greater good, Mom."

"Maybe." She didn't look convinced. "But does that individual have to be you?"

"If not me, Mother, who?" It wasn't easy, but I held my temper and started eating my lunch.

She didn't speak for a while. Finally, she couldn't hold back any longer. "Not all planets have overpopulation issues. Some are underpopulated."

"I know. But we're not talking about other planets. We're talking about Earth." I wondered where this was going.

"You could leave," she whispered.

I was so shocked that I stopped eating. "You want me to go away?"

"Of course I don't, Sophie. But you don't always get everything you want. I don't want you to have to deny yourself two of the most fundamental of human rights — a partner and a child. They can fulfill you in ways you can't even imagine."

Something she said triggered a memory: my Mom and Dad watching me open my birthday presents, beaming at each other and laughing together when I opened a box with my puppy in it. I knew she had sacrificed for me and that I brought her joy.

"I know, Mom. It's not like I don't want to get married. But we live in desperate times, and it's not responsible for someone like me to reproduce."

My mother narrowed her eyes and shook her head. "I don't understand you, Sophie. And I'd honestly rather lose you forever, knowing you were happy with a husband and a family on some strange planet far away than have you be alone forever on Earth." Her eyes teared up. "You know how much I would hate to have you go. That should tell you how strongly I feel about this whole Single for Life nonsense."

No answer would make a difference. We would never agree on this subject, and there was no point in trying to change her mind. If I wanted to stay on Earth, it was irresponsible and unethical to breed. I wouldn't do it.

When we finished eating, I stood up and put the plate with my unfinished food back in the fabricator for recycling. "I have to go to work, Mom. Thanks for lunch."

She kissed me and gently touched my cheek. "Just do one thing for me. Think about everything before you make a final commitment."

"My mind's made up, Mother."

"You're young, Sophie." Since she was looking directly at me, I refrained from rolling my eyes. "I'm afraid you will regret this."

"I won't regret it, Mom. Don't worry. I know what I'm doing."

I kissed her on the forehead and left, getting into a self-driving car parked on the side of the road and programming it for the Single for Life headquarters.

* * *

"And before these witnesses…"

My stomach was full of butterflies, and I had a moment of doubt. But as I stared out at the crowd of over two hundred people, I knew I wasn't going to back down. "I swear I will remain single for life and childless. My actions will help end overpopulation. I swear to…"

Suddenly, my mother's voice came back to me, making me forget what I was saying. *I'm afraid you will regret this.*

"…I swear to remain unmarried and barren. I will honor these words as long as I am on Earth."

The crowd erupted in cheers. They had taken the oath long ago and were here to welcome and support the people participating in the ceremony tonight. I sat down, but the cheering continued.

It was always exciting when one of the six regional leaders took the oath. I had put it off as long as possible, but when I got the promotion, I knew it was time. As the head of the North American division of Single for Life, I needed to lead by example. We weren't *required* to take the oath, but it was strongly encouraged.

At the reception, Nora Darwin came up to me and shook my hand. "Sophie McCallistair, that was a beautiful moment. You had such conviction in your voice! Sometimes, people sound like they aren't sure they want to be here, but your confidence in your beliefs came through loud and clear."

I beamed at her, still on a high from my public profession. "Thank you, Nora." Nora had started the movement long ago and continued to lead the entire organization. We had become close friends over the years.

"And congratulations on your new job," she added.

"Thank you. I can't wait to get started."

"Well, about that..." My heart skipped a beat. What did she mean? "The bank will finish processing the bonus into your bank account by tomorrow. I want you to use some of it for a vacation. Take a few weeks off."

"That will delay my start date."

"It's standard procedure, Sophie. You know that." *Shit.* I guess I did, but I hadn't focused on it. "You will be taking on some big responsibilities, and we always require people to have a cooling-off period before they begin their new positions. Don't you remember when you started as Regional Coordinator?"

Now that I thought about it, I did remember having to take a short leave right after I accepted that promotion. I didn't want to take time off now. I was ready to start. Earth was in trouble, and I wanted to jump right in and do everything I could to help.

I stepped closer and lowered my voice to a whisper. "Nora, is this necessary? I don't need a break. I want to start right away. There's a lot of work I need to do to hit my personal goals."

She patted me on the shoulder in her most motherly fashion. "I know you're ready to get started, Sophie. But I've seen a lot of people come and go. It's easy to burn out here, and a short, mandatory leave of absence is one of our requirements. We foresee you having a long and prosperous career with us as long as you don't crash and burn in your first five years."

I tried not to show how unhappy I was at this turn of events.

"Enjoy your time off. When you come back, you'll be rested and ready to start. Why don't you spend some time off-planet? They say Susohn is an excellent place to visit."

There was no getting out of it, so I nodded, but couldn't speak. I didn't want to cry in front of everyone.

* * *

Four hours later, I scanned my retina and waited for the security system to verify my identity before the door to my apartment slid open. After I had walked through, it shut behind me without a sound. "Lock." The mechanical whirring from the direction of the door indicated I was secure.

I had stood up in front of hundreds of people, and thousands more watching on video and declared my intention never to get married or have children, but this was not how I had expected to feel after taking my oath. When I had envisioned the event in my mind, I had thought I would feel triumphant. I had felt fantastic in the beginning. There was the excitement of declaring something in front of witnesses that I'd always believed in my heart. But in the aftermath, I felt dejected and depressed.

Maybe I did need a break. I stepped out of my clothes and stepped into the ionizer, standing there for the two minutes required for a thorough cleansing. When the timer went off, I got out and walked naked to my bedroom. The days of taking luxurious showers with water were long gone. Because of the wasteful habits of my ancestors, there was barely enough water left for the teeming population of Earth to drink.

I briefly wondered what it was like to take a shower — the kind I'd read about in books. I imagined water pouring over my head, trickling down and slowly heating up my body. That was one thing I might enjoy about interstellar travel; there weren't water shortages everywhere.

After I dressed in my pajamas, I set my BioScan on the floor and stood over it. It only took a few moments for the device to analyze my body completely. I picked it up and put it back on the shelf. The information would automatically upload to my computer.

I crawled into bed and pulled the covers up around me, opening the BioScan program to check my vital statistics.

Almost everything was within normal ranges. My cortisol was slightly elevated, from the stress of taking the vow, I supposed. The software would alert me if there were a significant change in my health that required emergency intervention. For any minor modifications, I had to monitor the numbers myself.

I called out to Teri, my virtual assistant, too tired to even bother swiping at my comm unit. "Teri, I need some help." The image of a young woman with short brown hair appeared on the floor in front of me. She wore casual blue jeans with an embroidered white peasant blouse. I'd have to see about changing that. I wasn't a fan of the retro look.

"Good evening, Sophie. What can I do for you?"

"Check my messages and see if Khellen has sent me anything. If there's a message, play it."

"No problem." She tapped her hand on her leg as she waited, accessing my information. I hadn't had a message from him for over a week. I kept expecting him to communicate at any time.

My patience was finally rewarded, and I could barely contain myself when Teri announced the message. A hologram from Khellen would chase away my disappointment and the uncomfortable feeling I'd gotten after taking the oath.

Teri activated the recording and disappeared as soon as it started playing. It felt like Khellen was sitting on my bed.

Technology had certainly progressed from the stilted 3D video files of my childhood to the point where a casual observer would think Khellen was here with me. He sat frozen, waiting for me to speak.

I suppressed the impulse to reach out and touch him. He was only an image, no matter how real he looked. But it didn't matter; I loved his messages. They were always cheerful and lighthearted. He never failed to make me feel better, no matter what was happening in my day.

Khellen was about my age and too handsome for his own good. He had brown hair, a cheeky grin, and eyes a peculiar shade of green that no baby on Earth had ever possessed. He had sent pictures of himself water skiing, swimming, and diving. I knew he liked the water, and all the physical activity gave him a toned body with washboard abs and well-developed biceps.

Frankly, the pictures made me envious. Water sports were little more than fairy tales on Earth. The oceans were so polluted that no one wanted to go into them. Any fresh water was reserved for drinking. I couldn't imagine having so much clean water that anyone could just play in it. It seemed wasteful.

"Hello, Khellen."

The hologram responded immediately. "How's it going, Sophie? I hope you're doing better than I am. You know how my mother has been pressuring me to get married? It turns out she was right. I probably should have made more effort to find a mate earlier." His voice

13

trailed off as he looked away from the camera. "I turn twenty-five in a couple of weeks. If I'm not married by then, I'm going to have some problems with the law."

This message wasn't cheerful at all. Khellen lived on Biyaha, where even though they had modern technologies and conveniences, their traditions were as old as the planet itself. Like Earth, Biyaha had a population problem. But it wasn't an overpopulation problem. It was the exact opposite. Their population started declining a century before. The government had passed laws encouraging people to have children in order to protect their future. At first, they gave parents monthly stipends for each child. When that wasn't enough, they enacted more draconian policies. Everyone who could bear children was required to get married by the age of twenty-five.

Khellen had told me that most got married as soon as they reached the age of majority, which was sixteen on Biyaha. Many young people didn't even have jobs because they could support themselves and their families on the government money. Instead, they chose to have more babies. Khellen had friends only a few years older than him with as many as six children. The government required couples to space their children at least two years apart because they didn't want the women weakened from too much childbearing.

The hologram had paused because its sensors showed I wasn't listening based on my eye movements, body language, and unresponsiveness. I thought about what Khellen had said. If he wasn't married by his birthday, he would become one of the disappeared. I shivered at the thought. No one was sure what became of people who vanished after their twenty-fifth birthday. There were rumors, of course. Death, torture, and breeding farms were some that Khellen had mentioned.

I had never thought he might become one of them. It couldn't be that hard, could it? Get married. That's all he had to do. He had no choice but to bow to the pressure his mother was putting on him. And I surely didn't blame her. I didn't want Khellen to disappear and never be seen again.

I had a feeling he had been searching for a woman who would be his perfect wife. Based on his worried expression, he hadn't found her yet. He had confided in me that he wanted to marry for love, but the government policy requiring marriage by twenty-five meant it wasn't always an option. Get married and breed. Those were the rules. Contraceptives were illegal on Biyaha.

I gazed at his unhappy face, wishing I could see him in person. Khellen was my best friend even though I had never been in the same room with him. We had encountered each other as teenagers at a virtual reality dance and had started corresponding soon after. We had been messaging each other for years since.

The hologram sensed me looking at it and resumed playback, but rewound a few seconds from where it had left off.

"If I'm not married by then, I'm going to have some problems with the law. The police will come and take me away. You know as well as I do what will happen after that. I won't be able to message you anymore, that's for sure, Sophie." He looked troubled, and his eyes lowered again.

I had never seen him act this way before.

"I should get married, right?" His odd green eyes stared into mine, or at least it felt that way.

"Yeah, you should, Khellen. Getting married can't be as bad as whatever the government does to those who don't comply." I spoke as if he could hear me.

"I know I should. But I don't feel like that would be the right thing to do, Soph." He stared off to the right as if he were thinking. "I'm going to hold off as long as I can. I'll figure something out." He paused to add quietly, "I wish we could talk." He held up his hands, a ghost of his usual grin on his face. "I know, I know, intergalactic vid comm rates are astronomical."

I nodded.

"Still..." He looked up then, and he must have been looking directly at the camera because his eyes stared right into mine. "I wish you were here."

The hologram winked out, leaving me bereft. I lay down, my heart so heavy I thought it would sink to the floor —

until I had a thought that lifted me back to a sitting position.

Khellen wanted me to come to Biyaha. I had two weeks off. And Nora said I should go off-planet.

Excitement set me tingling. I would go and visit him. We would finally get to meet, and I would convince him to get married so his government wouldn't knock him off or do whatever they did to those who broke the rules. I couldn't bear the idea of him disappearing. His messages brightened my days more than I wanted to admit. I couldn't take it if the holograms stopped one day.

I started getting excited. I was going off-planet for the first time in my life. Then I would come back and start my new job. Khellen would be married, and I would be single for life.

Both of us would get what we wanted.

CHAPTER 2

KHELLEN

"Mother, I'm going for a swim and then I'll be heading to town. I have errands to do." I hoped to sneak past while she was cooking. We had a fabricator to make meals, but she never used it. I was staying with my mother for the Mistivan season. This year, unfortunately, it coincided with my twenty-fifth birthday.

Mistivan is the main holiday on Biyaha, involving seven days of feasting, going to the temple, and visiting friends and family. We decorate the house and exchange gifts. It's usually my favorite time of year, but this time, I wasn't enjoying it very much. It was nearly over. After a few more days, I would be home again, and everything would go back to normal.

As long as I got married, of course. If I didn't, nothing would ever be normal again.

Still, having the lake nearby and Mom cooking all of my favorite meals almost made up for having to listen to her go on and on about me getting married. It's not like I didn't recognize the gravity of the situation. The government did not take it lightly when people defied the Edict of Marriage. And it's not that I didn't want to get married. I clung to the childish belief that I should marry a woman I loved.

Mom said that I would grow to love whoever I married, but I didn't believe her. I wanted to choose a partner myself. I had a vague idea of what I sought in a mate. I would recognize the right woman the moment I laid eyes on her. But I was running out of time, and part of me feared what the government would do to me if I didn't conform.

I was determined to put it off as long as I could, hoping that somehow the universe would bring a special someone to me. Lately, I'd been walking around all day long, trying to help the universe out a little bit, sizing up every woman I met and wondering if she was the one.

"Why don't you go up to the public beach?" My mom had her back to me. I could tell she was trying to sound casual and nonchalant. The public beach was probably full of beautiful young women looking for husbands. It would be like throwing myself to the sharks. But maybe she was right. I wouldn't meet anyone swimming here at our private beach.

"Okay, Mom. That's not a bad idea." She gave me a surprised glance. "I'll see you later."

I was already in my swim trunks, so I only needed to grab a towel from the walk-in closet near the door. As I walked across the lawn to the pathway leading to the beach, the computer on my arm flashed with an intergalactic message. It was Sophie. I grinned, stopping in the middle of the yard. It wasn't a hologram like usual, only text.

Khellen,

Sorry to hear you're still single. LOL. Hang tough. I'm sure whoever you marry will be the right woman for you, even if you don't think so at first. I have a nice surprise coming for you. Watch for it in a few days. Are you at your Mom's for Mistivan? I wish you were here instead. We'll meet someday. I just know it. In the meantime, keep those green eyes open looking for a wife. I have a Khellen message addiction, and I can't get by without your holograms, so stay alive for me, okay?

Take care. *blows a kiss*

I stared at the message for a moment as a familiar bittersweet feeling of loss swept over me. Sophie and I were good friends even though we lived a galaxy apart. Our correspondence had gotten me through some tough times and I always looked forward to her messages.

I smiled as I read it again. It was ironic that she was such a marriage advocate for me considering her job. Of course, Biyaha didn't have the same problems as Earth. I wondered what the surprise was. Knowing Sophie, she was sending me a wedding present. How could she afford the intergalactic postal fees?

It only took a minute to write back, telling her I was at my mother's place for the next few days. I would do my best to get married so she could keep getting her Khellen message fixes. Then I trotted off towards the beach, wondering if my dream woman was lying there in the sun waiting for me.

* * *

There wasn't anyone waiting for me on the beach. I did my twenty laps and went home. When I returned, my mother had put my breakfast aside.

"Khellen, you need to get dressed immediately." She sounded like I was ten and we were late for an important dinner.

"I know, Mom. I will. I'm capable of dressing myself."

"No, now. You have to be ready before temple. Someone's coming over."

"What kind of someone?" I was instantly suspicious.

My mother's eyes cut away from me. "A sweet girl. Don't be difficult, Khellen. I think she's the one."

"You think everyone's the one!" She made it sound like I was being picky about eating my vegetables, not choosing my wife.

"Look, she's pretty and willing to marry you. She looks like the one to me. Will you meet her, please?"

I was extremely reluctant, but I knew my mother was trying to help me. And part of me grew more fearful every day of what would happen when the government took me away.

We had a peaceful civilization and a mostly good government, but the Edict of Marriage wasn't something to ignore. People who didn't get married were never seen again.

I believed they were forced to breed in secret government facilities or taken to slave mines. Maybe it was something worse. The government deliberately left their fate vague enough so people would fill in the blanks with their worst fears. Whatever it was, though, everyone knew those people never saw their families again.

"Mom, it's not that I don't want to get married. But marriage is forever, and I don't want to be stuck with the wrong partner."

She shook her head. "Disappearing is also forever. You don't need to love her before you get married. You'll see, Khellen."

I wasn't sure. But I was willing to meet the woman my mother thought was good enough for me.

* * *

"Khellen, this is the girl I spoke about earlier."

"It's nice to meet you," Morda said. She looked more like a teenager than a grown woman. Mom mentioned she was twenty, but she was small and had a youthful face. I had the uncomfortable feeling that she had lied about her age, but I didn't know how much. We linked arms, with her holding my elbow in the palm of her hand and me holding hers — the traditional greeting on Biyaha. It was a typical introduction until the end, when she allowed her fingers to trail suggestively up my forearm, instead of releasing me immediately.

"It's nice to meet you, too." I gave her a quick once-over as we sat down. She was of medium build with large round breasts and curvy hips. Her face was pretty enough, I supposed. And she was sexy.

"Well, I'll leave you two to get acquainted." Mom smiled at me and nodded to Morda. There was a long, awkward silence after she left.

"So, what do you do for a living?" I figured an innocent question was polite and a good way to start.

"Khellen," she said, leaning forward and giving me an excellent view of her cleavage. I wondered if she was positioning her body this way on purpose. "We both know you don't have many choices right now."

I glanced up at her sharply.

"There's no point in treating this as a date when it's a business meeting."

I was taken aback and practically speechless. "That's an interesting way of looking at things."

"The only question that needs to be answered is whether we're compatible or not. I mean sexually. Why don't you come sit over here next to me."

"That seems a little aggressive," I said.

I was a virgin, of course. There was no sex outside of marriage on our planet. Despite the problems with underpopulation, this seemingly contradictory belief was part of our society. And everyone knew what the punishment for this was - death. There was nothing vague about it, unlike the disappeared.

The church on my planet was influential in our lives. Even as a modern society, we had some ancient laws still on the books. If you were caught, a lynch mob from your temple would come to your house to punish you and string you up.

When I was very young, I had seen a lynching. It didn't often happen, maybe every twenty years or so, but it was no empty threat. Everybody from the neighborhood was required to watch. The deterrent effect was powerful.

Males and females were separated during school and after-school activities until they turned sixteen. Then they were encouraged to marry immediately. The only reason I had met Sophie when I was fifteen was off-worlders had organized the VR camp. It would never have been allowed on Biyaha.

"We need to find out. Now come over here."

This woman's predatory ways were making me uncomfortable, but I had to admit she had a point. If we got married, the only reason would be to make babies, and that required sex. I supposed I would have to sacrifice. I got up and slowly walked over to where she was sitting on the couch. She scooted over, and I sat down. In a moment, she had my pants open and her hand inside. I gasped. I had thought we would start with a kiss.

"I see you're nice and pink. Pure for me," she whispered in my ear. And she did kiss me, but she also grabbed my cock firmly and began pumping her hand up and down. I kissed her harder, overcome by lust. No one had ever touched me there before.

With her other hand, she pulled up her shirt, and I saw that she was pure, too. Her breasts were pink, the color of someone from Biyaha, who has never had sex. If I had the opportunity to look between her legs, I knew her pussy would be pink down there, too. Once a person had sex, they would begin turning bright red, and the color got darker over the years.

The people of Biyaha were descendants of the Great Race, just like all the people in the Milky Way galaxy. Sophie's people on Earth were descendants of the Great Race, too, but there were small differences. For instance, I understood the sexual organs of humans lacked unique coloring. I didn't know why they ended up that way. On my planet, it was easy to tell if someone was a virgin. The color change only happened when skin met skin inside the woman and couldn't be triggered any other way.

She took my hand and put it on her breast. I didn't have any first-hand experience with women, but I had watched videos, of course. Without thinking, my hands started squeezing gently, and she moaned softly, pumping me harder and faster. I had lost the ability to reason and could think of nothing but the feeling of her hands on my cock when the computer on my forearm suddenly flashed with a message. Sophie's image popped into my head. I pulled my hands away from Morda immediately.

What was I doing?

I took my hand out of Morda's shirt and removed her hand from my pants, buttoning them up quickly.

"What's wrong? I thought you liked it."

I wasn't sure what to say. I knew saying *I was thinking of another woman* would be a mistake. "Morda, you know the law."

"We weren't breaking the law. My mother's a lawyer. I read up on it. It clearly defines penetration as the violation."

I felt myself turning red.

"I guess you got a taste of it," she said, shrugging. "What do you think? Are we compatible? Should we get married?"

I felt stunned as her tone changed. "Or do you want to disappear instead?" Her words brought the taste of fear to the back of my mouth. "We can do it every day. You know you liked it before your computer went off."

My comm unit. Sophie. Maybe she had written back. I checked the queue and was disappointed to see it was only a message that my bank statement had arrived.

I stared openly at Morda. She was not my dream woman. She was not someone in whom I was remotely interested. But beggars couldn't be choosers. And she would keep me from disappearing…which meant I could still write to Sophie.

I gave in. "Maybe my mother was right about you."

* * *

When we called my mom back into the room, she squealed and hugged both of us, grinning like a crazy woman. I guess she was excited and relieved because she had managed to save me — her only child — from disappearing from her life forever and had managed to secure grandchildren as well.

I wasn't nearly as excited. In fact, I felt like throwing up. I had always told myself I would marry for love. And now I was compromising my principles because I was scared. I knew the decision made sense. It was the logical, reasonable thing to do. But I wanted something different.

I wanted to feel the rush I'd heard about, where you feel so happy you could explode. I had wanted to love someone who loved me back. But the wheels were in motion now, and there was no going back. I was marrying Morda, whether I wanted to or not.

"So when's the date?" she asked casually.

"We're planning the wedding for the day before my birthday. I don't want to rush into this." I knew what my Mom was thinking. I had waited nearly ten years to get married, and that couldn't be considered rushing. I continued speaking as soon as I saw her start to open her mouth. "Morda's going to be out of town for a while. But she said she doesn't mind if you organize everything. Right?" I looked at her for confirmation, and she nodded. "We only want it small. Just a few people."

My mom had been delighted when I told her she would be allowed to plan the wedding, but her face fell when she learned she had to make it small. I held up a hand to forestall any further arguments. "Those are the conditions, Mom. Non-negotiable."

"That's all right. You tell me what you want, and I'll do it. I'll take what I can get."

* * *

A few days later, the sun rose as I headed for the water. I needed to move. I needed something to replace the enormous feeling of dread. The wind in the trees and the twittering of the early morning birds made me feel peaceful — something I hadn't experienced since I had met Morda.

I was staying at my mother's until the wedding and celebrations were over. It was more convenient to be around for the planning. I was down on the beach about to go into the water for my morning swim when I got a message from Sophie. Seeing her name made me smile for the first time since I had gotten engaged. Spending significant amounts of time with my fiancée had shown me that I liked her less the more I got to know her.

28

At least I wouldn't disappear. I held on to that because it was the only thing keeping me in the sham of a relationship.

I swiped the message. All it said was: Surprise!

What was that supposed to mean? I dove into the water and began doing laps out to the island and back. I pushed myself hard, trying not to think about my upcoming marriage or what Sophie's message could mean. But I couldn't get my mind off her communication.

Had she sent me something that would arrive today? I wasn't looking forward to getting it. It wasn't that I didn't want a present from Sophie, but it was sure to remind me that I was marrying a woman that I didn't even like to save my ass. I did ten extra laps, trying to work out my frustration, and eventually, I headed back to shore, still tied in knots.

I noticed a figure on the beach as I returned. It was still early. I had gone out in the dim light of predawn to have the beach to myself. It was private, but my mother liked to swim too. Usually, I would get up extra early so I could swim alone.

Who was on the beach, then?

There was no way my mother was up before her usual time. She was a late sleeper, to put it mildly. I kept swimming, trying to peer through my swimmer's eyelids. They were a technologically advanced version of goggles that helped improve my underwater vision.

When I got closer, I could make out that it was a woman. And she had red hair, not black, so it wasn't Morda. The swimmer's eyelids were supposed to allow you to see as clearly out of the water as in, but technology didn't always work as advertised. I was having trouble making out her features. She started digging in her bag, and her face became completely obscured.

I swam faster, intrigued by the stranger.

She seemed vaguely familiar. Why was she sitting on the beach as if she were waiting patiently for someone?

I reached shallow water finally and stood up, striding out of the lake towards the stranger. She stood up too, and her form and movements reminded me of someone.

"Khellen!" she called out. I tried to tear off the swimmer's eyelids as quickly as I could to get a good look at her. But they were stuck fast, probably because my hands were fumbling.

For some reason, I felt a strange excitement. It was like I was about to find something that had been missing or like a miracle was about to transpire.

Who did I know with that voice? I racked my brain, searching for a face to match the voice, but there was no one on Biyaha who sounded like that. I tore at the swimmer's eyelids, peeling each one off at last and looking up at the woman who now stood in front of me.

It couldn't be.

"Sophie?"

She smiled and threw her arms around me.

"Surprise."

CHAPTER 3

SOPHIE

Khellen's mother had directed me to the beach, which wasn't the reception I had envisioned in my mind. She knew Khellen and I corresponded, and I couldn't imagine why she would be less than pleased to see me. After all, I had come to encourage him to get married. She should be glad there was another ally around.

The path she indicated took me right to the water where I could see Khellen swimming out to an island. I sat down and waited for him to finish, feeling excited and eager to surprise him. There was some trepidation mixed in with the elation in my heart. What would it be like to finally meet him in person? Would it be awkward? Had I made a huge mistake?

It seemed to take forever for him to swim back. Then all of a sudden, there he was, standing up out of the water, trying to take his goggles off and having a hell of a time with them.

I stood up to greet him and froze. Khellen was…hot. There was no other word for it. I had pictures of how he currently looked, of course, but somehow I hadn't associated the images in my mind with reality. I had imagined he looked the same as when we had first met in that virtual reality camp years ago, and his physical presence was entirely different.

Back then he had been cute but skinny and awkward. There was an air of confidence about him now. He had a lean, powerful swimmer's body with broad shoulders and muscular biceps. His rock-hard abs tapered down to a narrow waist. His legs were well-muscled and robust. His hair was short and messy after his morning swim.

He was still adjusting his goggles when I started moving toward him, unable to wait for him to reach me. Finally, he tore them off, and by then I was standing in front of him.

He stared at me as if he had seen a ghost. "Sophie?"

Now that we were within arm's reach, I couldn't keep from touching him. I smiled and threw my arms around him. "Surprise," I said, holding him tightly.

His strong arms wrapped around me, and he nearly squeezed the breath out of me. Reluctantly, he let me go, and I stepped back. We grinned at each other until he finally spoke.

"How did you get here?"

"I got that promotion, remember? They always make us take occasional breaks to keep people from burning out. My time here is a vacation."

"But—"

"And they gave me a gigantic bonus," I added, answering the question I knew he was about to ask. "Which is how I could afford the flight out here."

"How long are you staying here?" He reached out for my hand as if he couldn't resist touching me, either.

"Until your birthday. I'll catch a ship out the next day."

"Oh." His smile fell.

"Is something the matter?" I sensed that beneath his happiness at seeing me, Khellen was uneasy about something. There was tension in every line of his body. "What is it?"

He bent down to pick up his towel, never letting go of my hand. He didn't bother to dry himself off. He simply threw the towel over his shoulder as we headed up the trail to the house, hand in hand.

"You came at an unusual time." He looked distraught and hesitated before he spoke again. "I'm getting married."

I felt a tightness in my chest, but ignored it. "That's good news," I said. Wasn't it? "I can't have you disappearing on me."

"No, I guess not." He tried to put a smile back on his face. "The wedding is the day before my birthday, so you'll be here for the festivities."

"Great." I dropped his hand. It didn't seem appropriate under the circumstances.

With visible effort, he corralled his usual good humor and gave me a grin. "So, Miss McCallistair, what should we do on your first day on Biyaha?"

"Do you have to ask?" I gazed longingly out at the water.

"Of course. I know the first order of business for a dehydrated human." He looked at me with an intense gaze I couldn't immediately identify.

"What's that?" A warm feeling spilled out of my heart when he looked at me like that.

"A shower, of course. Next a swim. Then a bath. And maybe some water sports later in the day. And if you want to be daring, take a second bath."

"Why are we wasting time talking about it, then?"

He laughed, knowing me and my fascination with water very well. "How about I take you back to the house to have your first shower, and then we'll get some breakfast. You can tell me about your trip."

"That sounds fantastic. I'm glad I'm here." I looked at him out of the corner of my eye, wondering if he was euphoric too.

He shook his head, beaming at me. "I can't believe you're here in the flesh. I was beginning to wonder if you were real, Sophie."

"Believe it." I reached out my hand and poked him in the chest. We headed back to the house, walking side by side up the path.

* * *

Khellen's mother met us when we came into the kitchen, deep in a conversation about my favorite music from Earth. The expression on her face looked stony. We stopped dead in our tracks, words trailing off to silence. She tried to paste a smile on her face, but it was unconvincing.

"Hi, Mom. This is Sophie." He looked so happy when he said my name that I practically melted inside again.

"Sophie, your pen pal?" She turned to me, confused. "You said you were a friend of Khellen's." Her tone was almost accusing.

"I am. We're friends, right Khellen?" I wondered where her attitude was coming from.

"Mother, I've shown you pictures of Sophie before."

"Those must have been taken quite some time ago." The way she looked at me now made me feel like a germ on a slide.

I tried to lighten the conversation, which seemed to be disintegrating in front of my eyes, but I didn't know why. "Oh, dear, did you show her the one from graduation?" Turning to him, I grimaced at the thought. At the time, I had acne, too-short hair, and twenty extra pounds. I hoped I looked considerably better now. "No wonder she didn't recognize me."

"You never said she was beautiful, Khellen." The words sounded like they could be a compliment, but she didn't seem in the mood to praise me.

Khellen looked upset and tried to end the conversation. "I didn't realize it mattered. You know what, Mom? Sophie's tired from her spaceflight and wants to get cleaned up. We'll see you later."

"Okay." As Khellen steered me out of his kitchen, she added, "But remember, your fiancée is coming over with her family for a party tonight before she leaves on her trip."

"That's right! I completely forgot about that for some reason. What time are they coming?"

"Eight o'clock."

"Got it." He showed me to the staircase. "Go up to the top and turn right. You can stay in the room at the end of the hall. I'll be around soon to show you how everything works. I need to have a word with my mother first, though. I'm sorry about her behavior."

"It's okay. Don't worry about it." I still wasn't sure what I had done to offend her.

He returned to the kitchen as I headed up the stairs. Almost immediately, I heard Khellen's voice escalate and his mother's screaming back him, and I paused. I knew I was eavesdropping, but I couldn't help myself from having ears.

"What was that, Mother?"

"What was that? What was that?" she repeated, shrill and exasperated. "What are you doing bringing a gorgeous girl like that into this house when you just got engaged? You're jeopardizing all my hard work?"

"Sophie has had an open invitation to visit me since I've known her. She decided to surprise me, and she's here in time for the wedding, which is great. I want her to be here. She's my best friend."

His mother snorted. "How can someone you've only talked with through holograms be your best friend? You're ridiculous."

"I'm getting tired of you meddling in my affairs." The longer he spoke, the louder he got. "Getting married was one thing, and I know you were only thinking about me. But stay away from Sophie. I won't have you interfering in my friendship with her or making her feel unwelcome."

"I don't understand what the fuss is about a little human from Earth."

There was a deadly silence, and I wondered how he would respond. The barb hit home. I knew some aliens considered humans lower-class citizens in the universe, but I didn't know Khellen and his family thought that way.

"If you think I'm making a fuss, I'll go home. I don't have to stay with you. I'm here because I usually enjoy it, and I know you like having me around. But if you're going to disrespect Sophie, I will not stay under your roof." His voice had a note of steel in it that I had never heard in his hologram messages.

"You would leave and miss out on spending Mistivan at home because of her?" Her tone was incredulous.

"Yes. As I said before, she's my best friend, and you've insulted her several times in a single conversation. It's inexcusable."

There was silence again, and then I heard Khellen burst through the door into the hallway, looking furious. He froze when he saw me standing on the stairs.

I put on my most apologetic face. "I'm sorry. I didn't mean to listen in on your conversation. I just wanted to find out why she doesn't like me."

Before Khellen could speak, his mother came in after him. "Khellen, please, don't go." She broke off when she saw me standing in front of her and realized that I had heard everything. Her face went blank, and she drew a deep breath. "I'm sorry for what I said, and I would like you both to stay."

Khellen scowled. He was still upset with his mother, and I was severely embarrassed.

"Sure, it's fine," I said.

Khellen turned to her. "It's not fine, Mother. But we'll stay, for now."

She blinked and looked confused. I was confused too. I had never seen this side of Khellen before, and I realized that even though I felt closer to him than anyone else, we hardly knew each other. I followed him up the stairs, leaving his bewildered mother behind. For the first time since my shuttle had blasted off from Earth, I wondered what the hell I was doing.

* * *

Khellen's legs looked stiff and jerky as he climbed the stairs, with none of the grace I had seen earlier when he emerged from the water. He was quite upset, and I wanted to reassure him that I wasn't offended.

"Khellen." I put my hand on his arm to make him look at me. He stopped. "It's okay. I'm sure she means well."

He cut me off. "I don't understand her. You have to know that she has a kind heart. I don't know why she's acting like this."

"I want you to know that I'm not offended."

He looked at me skeptically.

"Do you think you're the first aliens who don't like people from Earth? I've had run-ins with people from other planets before."

"There are others who've treated you this way?" He seemed disturbed by the idea.

"Just a couple of jerks on the flight. Nothing to be upset about."

"It's frustrating."

"Why?" I looked up into his green eyes, and for a second it felt like my heart skipped a beat.

"Because." He hesitated, and it seemed as if he couldn't tear his eyes away from mine. "You're my friend."

"Oh." I was disappointed in his answer, even if I couldn't say why. I was his friend, wasn't I?

"Anyway, this is a towel. It's for drying off your body."

I rolled my eyes. "I know what a towel is, Khellen."

He smiled briefly, but it didn't reach his eyes. As he led me into a small bathroom connected to my room, he continued his explanation. "This is your shower." I peeked around his body into the stall. "You swipe your hand over this pad. Blue will make it colder, and red will make it hotter. Take as long as you want. We have too much water in the lake this year; they're going to have to drain some of it. Knock yourself out."

"Okay." We were standing only inches apart, partially inside the shower stall, and my heart started to race. I glanced up at Khellen, wondering if he was as affected by our proximity as I was. I stepped away quickly and bumped into the wall. "Got it. I'm sure it will be wonderful."

"Call if you need any help." He looked lost. "Not cleaning yourself. I mean, if you can't get it to work. I mean…"

I laughed, and the spell broke. His cheeky grin came back, and he gave me a quick peck on the cheek before he left.

I had always thought that a shower would be like standing in the ionizer, only wetter. I was wrong. Once I got the temperature adjusted and stripped off my clothes, I slipped under the shower and let the water stream down my body. It was the most amazing feeling I could remember. Everything was warm, and the water moving over my body was a sensual experience.

The water spilled everywhere, and my nipples hardened when I turned them into the solid stream of water. The sensation made me think of Khellen, but I tried to force my mind elsewhere. He was getting married, and I was not. I had taken a vow.

I had a boyfriend before I joined Single for Life. We fucked, but we were young, and he had never been able to last long enough for me to come. I always pretended I was having an orgasm and then finish myself off later. I didn't want to hurt his feelings. But ever since I joinedSingle for Life, I had tried to put aside all physical desires and focus on my goal of saving the Earth from overpopulation one person at a time, starting with myself.

Something in my head reminded me that there was no overpopulation problem on Biyaha. They *wanted* people to have babies here. But I wasn't staying here forever. I was going home soon, and Khellen was going to marry a beautiful girl who would make him happy. At the very least, she would keep him from disappearing.

I regretfully turned off the water. It had been one of the most incredible experiences of my life, and I wished it had gone on forever. I took consolation in the fact that I could shower plenty while I was off-planet.

I stepped out of the shower and started toweling myself off. I nearly came in there. Who knew that getting clean could be so pleasurable? It almost made me feel guilty. There was nothing sensual about using the ionizer. You stepped in dirty and stepped out clean.

"Sophie? You okay in there?" Khellen's voice through the door made me blush. I was still naked, and I looked at myself in the mirror. Medium breasts. Flat stomach. Slim legs. Attractive face. Long copper-colored hair. Blue eyes. Not a devastating beauty, that was for sure. I wondered what his mother had seen in me.

I was pretty enough, I supposed. Not that it mattered. For a brief moment, I wondered if Khellen thought I was pretty. What did it matter? We were only friends. I watched my cheeks turning a rosy pink in the mirror.

"Sophie?"

I realized that I hadn't answered him even though I was thinking a lot. "Oh, yes. I'm fine. The shower entranced me."

"I have your bag here if you want some clean clothes."

That would mean opening the door with only a towel covering me and Khellen standing right in front of me. The thought sent a thrill straight to my core, and my breath quickened.

"I'll just leave it out here." I felt irrationally disappointed that he wasn't going to be there.

I eased the door open and peeked out. No Khellen and that was probably for the best. I grabbed my bag and dragged it into the bathroom, pulling out some shorts and a T-shirt. I needed to get some clothes on. Nudity was playing tricks on my mind. When I emerged from the bathroom, I went to look for Khellen and found him in his old bedroom. I recognized it from his holograms before he moved into his apartment.

"All clean?"

I blushed again, turning away and pretending to look at something on his dresser so he wouldn't see my red cheeks. "Totally. What are we going to do now?"

"How about this? I packed us a picnic, and I thought I'd take you out in the boat."

I turned to face him, hoping my cheeks had settled down. "That sounds fantastic. Are you sure I'm not intruding on anything?" I had to be sure after the reception I had gotten from his mother.

"No." His voice suddenly sounded too loud, and he dropped it to a more reasonable tone. "I'm glad you're here, Sophie. I felt like I was alone for a while, and now that you're here, it's like I have someone who's on my side."

"I am, Khellen. But there's another woman in your life now." I didn't want to ask anything overtly, but I was extremely curious about her.

His expression darkened. "You'll see when you meet her." He went over to a window and stared out at the wisps of yellow clouds drifting by in the green sky. "She's no Sophie," he muttered under his breath.

Why was he comparing his fiancée to me? I needed some time to think and sort things out. Since I had gotten here, my mind felt hazy and dizzy. The only clear thing I could see was Khellen. But I knew that wasn't my future. We would both soon be married: He to a woman. I to my cause. There was no room for anything but friendship between us. I decided I would reassess my situation when I got into bed in the evening. Until then, I just had to keep myself out of trouble.

Khellen turned around and gave me a smoldering, tormented look. I felt a primal energy tingling throughout my body again. Maybe keeping out of trouble would be harder than I thought with Khellen around.

CHAPTER 4

KHELLEN

I stared at myself in my bedroom mirror, wondering who the person was I saw staring back at me. I imagined myself to be a hard-working, stable, and reasonable person. It was unheard of for me to give my mother backtalk or threaten to leave her house in the middle of the Mistivan season.

My pale, sky green eyes stared back at me. I shook my head silently. Ever since Mother had insisted that I meet Morda, my life had taken an unexpected turn. Sophie's arrival made me feel even more confused. It was a pleasant surprise, but I didn't understand my reactions to her. Her presence made my impending marriage seem like a rash decision.

Looking away from my image, I cursed myself for not having tried harder to find someone when I was younger. Now it was too late, and I was stuck with the bottom of the barrel. No, that was unkind. Morda would make the perfect wife for someone. Just not for me.

Maybe I could talk to Sophie about it. She always had a level head when it came to giving advice, and she hadn't steered me wrong before, except for when she advised me to get married. Even that hadn't been bad advice. The concept was sound; it was the fiancée who was the problem.

I wondered if I could find someone else at the last minute. Of course not. It had taken my entire lifetime to find Morda. Besides, I had given her my word, and I was reluctant to go back on it because I made a hasty decision. I would have to spend the rest of my life with that woman. The thought of waking up beside Morda every day forever was beginning to make me feel ill.

Back to square one. If the impossible happened, and I found a more suitable woman in the next day or so, I would call it off with Morda, I promised myself. The dreamlike fantasy made me feel better right away. I made such a terrible mistake getting engaged to Morda. What was I thinking?

I closed my eyes and tried to calm down. When I opened them again, I checked myself in the mirror. Did I look okay? My hair was in its usual half-messy state after I combed it with my fingers and half-heartedly pushed it into place. Women seemed to like it that way. Even if I brushed it and combed it, after five minutes on The Boat it was going to look the same, so what was the point of meticulous grooming?

I had on a pair of shorts and a T-shirt. My biceps filled out the arms of the shirt well. I had spent many hours swimming to earn them, and I liked how I looked. Maybe I should have shaved, but frankly, after an hour or two on the boat, I would have a five o'clock shadow again. I wasn't trying to impress Sophie or anything.

We were good friends, and we were going to have a pleasant afternoon hanging out on The Boat. I had many questions to ask her about herself and Earth. You couldn't get to know someone messaging the same way you could when you're face-to-face.

I grabbed my bag and headed down the hall to Sophie's room, knocking on her door. She answered immediately, and I lost my breath when I saw her. She had pulled her long copper hair into a ponytail, giving her a saucy look. She wore white short shorts that showed off her long legs and a white-and-yellow-striped top. Her blue eyes were smiling at me, and I stared, unable to form words. I saw what looked like bikini straps on her shoulders and latched on to the only thing I could think of to say. "Got your bathing suit on?"

"Yep. But I don't know if I want to go swimming."

"No swimming?" I pretended to be aghast as I struggled to regain my senses. "You know that's a critical part of enjoying the water, right?"

"Don't judge me." She ducked her head. "I don't know how."

"It's easy." I tried to remember a time when I learned to swim, but couldn't. I think I was three when I started lessons. "You'll pick it up quickly. I won't let anything happen to you."

"We'll see. But I can get some sun at least, right?"

"You certainly can." I felt my cock begin to stir at the thought of Sophie in a bikini and casually shifted my body so she couldn't see anything. "We should get going. We have to be back here by seven. The party starts at eight."

We walked down the hallway, and Sophie angled her head to catch my eye. "This is the party for Morda?"

"Not exactly. Mother's arranged a hover party. She loves them. They're impossible to describe without spending half an hour doing so. It's something you have to experience for yourself."

"Sounds interesting, but I'm having second thoughts about the boat, Khellen."

"Don't worry. I have a life band for you. It will help you relax. I don't want to get all scientific, but you wrap it around your neck, and it creates a force field around your body that makes you more buoyant."

Mom was out, so we locked up the house and headed down to the dock. The day was warm and sunny with a bit of a breeze to cool us off. The forest provided us with welcome shade from the sun.

"I imagine this is what Earth was like before we ruined it." Sophie looked wistful. "Beautiful forests — though our plants are green, not purple. A gorgeous, bright blue sky. A green sky still makes me feel loopy."

I smiled, unable to imagine a blue sky. I had never been off-planet. "Lots of clean water."

When Sophie saw The Boat, her eyes widened. The Boat is still impressive, even to me. Dad had her built to his exact specifications fifteen years ago before he died. She was about twenty feet long, with a shaded part at one end that housed some comfortable couches and chairs for lounging out of the sun.

The other end had a control panel for piloting, a diving board, and a ladder into the water mounted on the side. In between was a recreational area. There were long, cushioned benches along the sides where people could lie and sunbathe, and in the middle of the open space was a high table perfect for conversation and eating.

We called her The Boat, but she was actually a hovercraft that skimmed two or three inches above the water when she was moving and floated on the water when she wasn't. It was perfect for parties, hanging out in the middle of the lake, or fishing.

"This is what you're calling 'The Boat'?" She stepped onto the deck, trailing her fingers along the smooth, handcrafted railing.

"It's a vehicle that moves on the water. Were you expecting something different?"

"I was picturing a little wooden rowboat or a metal motorboat like in the stories I've read. Not a massive party house." She waved her hands helplessly at The Boat.

I pretended to be nonchalant but was secretly quite pleased. "To be precise, it's a hovercraft. But it floats when it's at rest."

"I suppose," Sophie said, moving towards the shaded area.

"Please put this on and activate it before we head out."

She looked back at me doubtfully. Now I began to understand that she was frightened of the water.

"You'll be fine." I handed her the band, which she wrapped around her neck. It faded so I couldn't see it. But when she turned towards me, the sun reflected off it, giving a shimmer in the light. "There's nothing to worry about now that you are wearing the life band. You certainly can't drown while you're wearing it, and I won't let anything happen to you. You're protected twice."

"Do I have it on correctly?" She still looked concerned.

"Perfect. Now let's get out there. We can talk the whole afternoon away on the water."

She stepped onto The Boat and kicked off her sandals immediately. While I got The Boat started, Sophie wandered around, gripping handrails wherever she could. I planned to take a short cruise and then see if I could convince her to go for a swim.

"What's happening with Single for Life?" While I talked, I pressed the button to uncouple The Boat, releasing her from the mooring at the dock. I steered her along the shore, and we started to cruise gently over the water.

"I have no idea. I haven't even thought about work since I got here." She looked embarrassed.

"You're on vacation. You're not supposed to be thinking about work, are you?"

"That's true." She crossed the deck and joined me at the steering console. "I still feel guilty. My work is my life back home."

"Tell me all about it. We have the whole day."

"I'm going to catch some sun while I can. It's still spring back home, and I'm pretty pale."

"Sure." I held my breath as she pulled the tank top over her head. She was facing away from me, and her string bikini left her back completely bare except for the thin straps. I closed my eyes. Give me strength.

Next, she shimmied out of her shorts, and I watched them fall down those endless legs. It was a good thing I was standing behind the console because I didn't want her to see how she was affecting me. We were just friends. And I was getting married; I couldn't let myself be attracted to Sophie.

She folded her clothes and then turned around, coming back toward me. She seemed like she wasn't self-conscious, but I noticed her cheeks were turning pink. The view of her body from the front was even better than her rear, and I averted my eyes so it wouldn't seem like I was staring. Her breasts looked round and perky, and I could see her nipples standing upright at attention. It was too much, so I turned my gaze to the shore as she spoke.

"Here's the thing about Single for Life. I don't know how to explain it, but I feel like I'm making a difference for Earth. The overpopulation problem is getting desperate. Our world leaders are considering requesting refugee status and shipping some of our students off-world. If we could just stop having babies, it would help even more."

A vision popped into my head of Sophie, her belly round and full with a gentle smile on her face. The image was sweet and erotic at the same time, making me question myself. My mouth didn't say the words that were in my head. "That's right. Stop having babies."

"Yes. We have actuaries in the organization who have run the numbers, and Earth's best hope is to convince young singles to stop getting married."

"That sounds like something difficult to sell. Doesn't everyone want to get married and have babies?"

She shook her head. "There are lots of people, like me for instance, who don't want that."

I instantly felt something was wrong. For Sophie to never get married and never hold her child in her arms? That wasn't a universe in which I wanted to live. "You don't want to get married or have kids?" I asked. "You never told me that before."

"I hadn't made a firm decision before, but now I have. I took my vows right before I left Earth."

"What was in this vow, exactly?" I was starting to feel sick to my stomach.

"We get people to commit to the single life, and we provide support for individuals who choose to live differently. We organize events and provide counseling when those who remain single run into any social difficulties."

"You sound like you're reading from a script." She blushed again, and I chuckled.

"Sorry, I get carried away sometimes. Work is my life."

Her words sounded sad to me, but they seemed to make Sophie happy. "What's this vow, though? You didn't explain it."

"I don't know it exactly, but it's something like this…" And she started to recite: "Before these witnesses, I swear to remain unmarried and barren for my entire life. I will keep my vow for the whole of my life on Earth."

"Wow. That's certainly unique." Words escaped me.

She wrinkled her nose. "I know it might sound crazy to you, but if you could see the conditions people are living in on Earth, I'm sure you would understand. Poverty, resource wars, crowded cities, pollution…there's nothing like this left." She gestured around at the idyllic scene.

I didn't say anything. The picture she painted was a difficult concept for me to understand.

"Really! It's all concrete, power lines, and garbage."

"Garbage?" I stumbled over the strange word. Most races in the galaxy spoke Standard, but some words are never used on certain planets.

"Garbage," she said, grimacing. "You know, stuff you throw out. A bag from the store. The packaging on food. A piece of paper you don't need anymore."

"Don't you reconstitute?" The thought of junk flying around in the streets was disgusting.

"We fabricate our food, but I can't imagine eating a newspaper."

"You don't eat it. At least, you don't eat the things that are inedible. You put plastic in the machine and make new plastic things out of it. Or you put food scraps in, and they get turned into compost, and you grow new food from it. I don't think we have what you call 'garbage' here."

"You're lucky." She looked kind of hopeless, so I put my hand on her shoulder and squeezed. I told myself it was to comfort her and not because I wanted to touch her smooth skin.

"It can't be that bad on Earth, can it?" Reluctantly, I took my hand away.

Her brow furrowed. "You don't understand, Khellen."

Then she flipped over her arm, showed me the screen on her computer. The images of poverty, pollution, and the crowded conditions in which people lived repulsed me. Was that where she came from? It was clear that I hadn't understood the extent of the problems on Earth.

"I don't live like this, you know. But how can I go about my comfortable life knowing other people are suffering? I have to do something, Khellen, and what I'm going to do is stay single."

I studied her quietly as The Boat made its way slowly down the lake. A gentle breeze ruffled her hair, and her eyes looked bright and ardent. Sophie was amazing, and I was fortunate to have her as a friend. "That's surprisingly noble." I didn't know what to say. "Do you think your ideals help convince other people to do the same thing?"

"I hope so." A tiny smile played over her lips as she thought about her work. "Now that I've taken the oath, my word will mean even more because it shows my commitment."

"But Soph," I said, swiping at the console to turn The Boat and head back around toward the island.

"Yeah?" She crossed the deck and lay face down on one of the benches. She put her towel under her head and closed her eyes.

"Did you ever want to fall in love? Get married? Have a family?"

"Maybe when I was a little girl." She fell silent, then propped herself on her elbows so she could look at me in the face with her intense blue eyes. "But that was a long time ago. I have to make adult decisions now. We can only stop overpopulation by limiting population growth. And since the government isn't willing to commit to legislation, the people of Earth have to start a grassroots movement. That's my life, and I like it."

"Hey, I'm not saying you're wrong." I tilted my head as she stared at me, her eyes unsettled. "Who are you trying to convince, Sophie? Me? Or you?"

She scowled at me. "I'm happy with my life, Khellen. My work is everything, and I don't need anything more."

I made myself busy turning The Boat. If I said another word, I might get something thrown at my head. I heard her huff out her breath, and when I turned back she was lying with her head turned away from me.

It seemed like a waste to have a beautiful, intelligent, sexy woman like Sophie single for life. She should be loved. And she ought to hold a sweet, innocent baby in her arms and feel a mother's love. She ought to have her round, perky breasts droop and stretch to feed her child. She should grow old with a family around her that loved her.

I gazed at her, having difficulty comprehending why I felt so upset. It wasn't right, but it also wasn't my decision. It wasn't my life, and we were only friends. There was nothing I could do about any of it. She had made her choice and had to live with it. I would have to live with it, too. Not that it affected me - my wedding was a week away. Sophie would go back to her filthy, crowded planet, and her job saving it from itself. I couldn't change that.

But why did it feel like something was wrong?

CHAPTER 5

SOPHIE

We came back from the lake earlier than we planned, so I had time to get ready for the evening's party without rushing. I nervously checked my credit balance. There was enough left from my bonus for me to get a fancy dress.

I thought Khellen's mother had only invited me because she didn't have a choice. She probably assumed I would show up in inappropriate clothes and make Khellen's fiancée look even better. I'm not sure why it was so important to me to prove her wrong. Maybe it was on behalf of everyone on Earth who had aliens look down on them. Maybe I wanted to show her that I wasn't someone to be forgotten from a low-class planet. Or maybe it was because she was acting like a bitch, and I wanted to see the look on her face when I appeared at her party looking like a movie star.

I was disappointed in myself for having that last thought. I didn't want his mother to hate me. I was trying to like her for Khellen's sake, but she didn't make it easy. Perhaps she would like me better if I could impress her.

"Teri, I need help." Time for some help from my virtual assistant. She appeared before me this time in a lavender, lightweight summer dress.

"How can I assist you, Sophie?"

"I'd like a dress for a party."

"Sure." She snapped her fingers.

I immediately found myself sitting on a bench in the empty virtual construct of a store. "Biyaha high fashion. Find dresses for a fancy party."

"Sure, Sophie. Do you want me to choose an outfit for you?"

I thought about it. "Not today, Teri, thanks."

"Okay." She vanished immediately. I wondered if she sounded disappointed or if it was only my imagination. I had to stop attributing human emotions to my assistant. It wasn't healthy.

The store populated with hundreds of dresses. Way too many for me to decide. Maybe I needed some help after all. "Match my coloring. Something in green," I called out.

Most of the dresses instantly disappeared, and I was left with a bunch of green dresses along with a few others in colors that might match my pale skin, blue eyes, and red hair.

"Hm." I stood up and started looking through them. "Remove all the dresses that end above the knee."

The selection dwindled.

"Form fitting and long," I added.

After narrowing the selection, there was a reasonable number for a person to look through. I found five that I liked and tagged each one, sending them to my closet until I was ready to wear them.

My first selection appeared on my virtual body. I moved around in it a bit, walking back and forth in the store before deciding I didn't like the cut.

"Let me see the next one instead." Another dress appeared on my body. I had gone through two more before I found the perfect dress. It was forest green and made my eyes and hair stand out. The floor-length, off-the-shoulder sheath hugged my curves tightly and flared out at the hem, right below my knees. I appraised myself in the mirror and decided I looked fantastic.

I couldn't see my feet, so I chose a pair of sensible flats in the color of the dress. I had the program arrange my hair in an elegant French twist and smiled at my reflection. Perfect. Khellen's mother wouldn't know what hit her.

I sent my purchases to the household 3D printer. I would do my hair and then go down in a half an hour to see if they were ready. I was excited and felt a little like a princess going to the ball. In the back of my mind, I hoped Khellen would enjoy my appearance. Part of me was surprised that I couldn't stop thinking about Khellen that way.

We're just friends, I told myself. *Get over it*. It seemed much easier to think the words than act upon them.

* * *

An hour later, I was ready to go, pacing around my room, waiting for Khellen to come and get me. We were supposed to go down to the party together, and he would introduce me to everyone.

There was a knock at my door, and I stood up, taking a deep breath. *Here goes nothing*, I thought.

When I opened the door and saw Khellen standing there, my breath caught in my throat. His eyes swept down my body and back up, locking onto me with a heat that made me tingle. He looked unbelievable. I had never been so close to a man who was that handsome. He wore a black suit cut in the latest Biyaha style. The shirt under his coat was the same mint green color of his eyes and the sky.

I suddenly remembered how he had looked in the morning coming out of the water. And then I had a new image of his strong, hard body pressing me down into my bed. I drew in a ragged breath and attempted to gather my scattered thoughts. I thought I had only drifted off for a few seconds, but it made me uncomfortable to have such thoughts about a soon-to-be-married man.

Also, I was single for life. Had I forgotten about that?

It wasn't a vow to forswear sex, but there was an unacknowledged recommendation at the organization that celibacy was probably for the best. It kept our primal urges at bay and ensured that no unexpected pregnancies occurred. Artificial birth control had improved by leaps and bounds over the years, but we had never been able to make it a sure thing. There was always a non-zero failure rate that meant somebody was going to get pregnant.

I had managed to abstain from sex since I had joined. Before that, there had only been one boyfriend in college. I had been sexually active for about ten months out of my adult life, and that was six years ago. Of course, I wanted sex sometimes. I didn't need to have it. But I was starting to think it was because I hadn't been around the right person before. When I looked at Khellen in his suit, seeing his eyes and remembering his body from the morning, I felt flushed with want and need.

I needed to say something before I embarrassed myself. "You look good," I blurted out.

Was that the best I could do? I was drawing attention to how sexy he looked and how I was slobbering over him. I hoped I wasn't drooling.

He swallowed, and I watched in fascination as his Adam's apple bobbed in his throat. "You do too," he said, looking dazed.

"Ready to go?"

And everything suddenly snapped back to reality. "Of course." I followed him into the hall. "I see you found a dress, Soph. You look beautiful, but maybe too beautiful. You might have had some pity on the men at the party."

He said the last sentence with a straight face, holding out his arm for me. I felt a bit like royalty as I hooked my arm through his and proceeded down the spiral staircase. "What do you mean?"

"Sophie, my dear, you are going to give all the gentlemen whiplash with that dress."

I didn't say anything, but I could feel my cheeks getting red. Wasn't that the point? To give one man whiplash, at least.

I reminded myself to get my mind out of the gutter. *He's engaged. And you've vowed to be single for life.* What was it about Khellen that made me forget everything?

We went out the front door, and when we arrived at the side of the house, there was a big pile of discs large enough to comfortably stand on. These must be the hover pads. Each disc had a transparent railing for safety. I stepped through the open gate of one and secured it behind me. Khellen did the same. I gripped the handrail tightly as the disc bobbed gently under my weight.

"I assumed you haven't used one of these before, human."

I shook my head, suddenly feeling anxious.

"It's not difficult, but you have to trust the pad. To turn, all you need to do is lean into it." He demonstrated by shifting his weight to the right, and he started drifting lazily in that direction. Then he moved his weight to his left foot and floated back to me. "To go up, you pull on the railing."

"And you push on the railing to come back down?" I spoke up, trying not to look scared.

"That's right. There's an altitude failsafe, so if you go too high, the computer will automatically bring you straight back to the ground. If you have any trouble, press the red button with your foot. That will create a force field around you. If you fall, you'll bump softly against the ground instead of crashing into it."

"Okay," I said, clinging to the railing of my hover pad.

"You don't look okay."

"Well, I'm not always good with heights. But I'll figure it out." I took a deep breath. Maybe this was going to be fun.

"Let's go!" He leaned forward on his hover pad, and it drifted to the back of the house. I did the same, feeling my disc slowly floating forward. The ambling speed made me feel safe. The breeze in my face was welcome because it was turning out to be a hot night.

When we came around the house into the enormous field they called a backyard, I gasped in amazement. Khellen's mother certainly knew how to throw a party.

There were five different levels in the air. A different color of floating lights set apart each level from the others. The ground level had food and drinks as well as comfortable seating for those who didn't want to fly around in the air. There were also a solid dance floor and a band playing quiet music.

On the second level, which was blue and offset from the ground level, was a hover pad dance floor in midair. Some people held hands and swayed to the music that floated up to them.

The third level — it was purple — had floating counters offering various activities for people to amuse themselves. Some people were already blowing bubbles. Others were tossing balls at a hoop. It reminded me of basketball, but the balls didn't fall when they missed the target; they hovered in the air until someone picked them up.

Still other guests were stepping off their hover pads and onto an enormous invisible platform in the air. They were bouncing up and down on what appeared to be nothing at all, but it was probably a force field.

The next level up, which boasted yellow lights, had floating tables and chairs with board games. Two men were playing a game that looked similar to chess. Another couple lazily moved pieces on an unfamiliar game board while keeping their eyes glued to each other all the time.

The final level had green lights and what looked like puffy, floating clouds. There were only two people up there, and they were lying back gazing at the stars. Hovering near another cloud was a telescope.

Beyond the gathering, I could see the island in the middle of the lake. As the sun set and the two moons rose, the sky changed from light green to dark green, to blue, to purple. The colors were breathtaking. I took in the view with people floating around from level to level, the music playing, and the lights. I felt my mouth drop open. Khellen was watching me, and I glanced at him briefly and back to the spectacle before me. "You could have prepared me better."

"Do you like it, then?" His eyes were warm, and a similar warmth filled my chest.

"It's spectacular. I've never imagined anything like it."

His mother appeared on a hover pad in a black, knee-length dress that showed off her trim figure. "Oh, Khellen, there you are. Hello, Sophie." She looked me over. "I see you found a dress."

"The stores on this planet are excellent." The uncomfortable feeling I got around her crept back into my head.

"That's nice," she said, but her face told me she was anything but pleased. "Enjoy yourself. Morda will be here any minute. I'll message you to come and greet her."

"Sure, Mom." Khellen's voice was carefully neutral.

She nodded and moved her hover pad away from us.

"Come on," he said. "Let's go up to the top level. You can get an unobstructed view of the stars from up there."

I looked up. "I don't know, Khellen, it looks pretty high."

"Come on, trust me." He held his right hand out and kept hold of the railing with the other.

"Do you want me to let go?" I stared at his hand as if it were a snake.

"Sophie." His gentle tone made me melt. Trembling, I released my hand and reached out to him. He took my hand and held it firmly. "Now pull up with your other hand."

I followed his instructions, and we rose slowly together. I looked around as we rose above everyone else's heads. Khellen's mother watched us from the ground with a disapproving look on her face. I didn't care. Holding his warm, steady hand was pure pleasure. I felt the energy flowing from where our hands were connected, and it filled me with peace.

We arrived on the star-gazing level as the other people were leaving, so we had it to ourselves. He found a large, fluffy-looking cloud, and we nudged our hover pads until we were directly above it. A light breeze was blowing, pushing clouds across the two moons, so the lights flickered in and out of view.

"Open your door and step down onto the floater," he said.

I bit my lip nervously at the thought of getting off the hover pad now that I was actually in a comfortable position.

"Never mind. I'll get out first." He let go of my hand and opened his railing, stepping down onto the cloud. "See? Nothing to be afraid of."

I opened the fence and hesitated, still a little scared. "Come on." Khellen held his hands out, and I took them, setting one foot down carefully on the cloud. But the surface was uneven, and I stumbled, falling into Khellen, who wrapped his arms around me and carefully caught me.

I closed my eyes and breathed in his aroma. I felt his arms and warmth around me. I knew then that I wanted him desperately.

I took a shaky step back, pushing away from his body. Down that road lay madness. I couldn't have Khellen; he was getting married. *You can't have something just because you want it, Sophie. That's not how life works.*

"Sorry about that," I said.

"Don't be," he answered. "I'll always catch you if I can." His response made my longing worse. I turned away from him.

"I don't know how I'm going to sit down here. This dress may look good, but it isn't practical." That was my best effort at a neutral topic of conversation.

"The floater conforms to your body shape. As long as you make yourself comfortable, it will support you in any position."

"Really?" It was technology we didn't have on Earth.

"Try it for yourself."

I sat down awkwardly and leaned back. The cloud supported me as securely as if I were lying back in a comfortable chair. "This feels great," I said, staring up at the stars.

"Earth is over there." He pointed off to the right.

I looked where he indicated, but all the stars looked the same to me. To my surprise, I didn't even feel the desire to be on Earth. I didn't feel any homesickness whatsoever. "I don't miss it at all, Khellen." As soon as I said the words, my lack of feelings for my planet began to bother me. "That can't be right. If you left here, you'd want to come back home, wouldn't you?"

"Of course I would."

"Is there something wrong with me?" I was asking myself as much as him. "It isn't a paradise like Biyaha, but it is home."

"We have a saying here. 'A home is made where the heart is laid.'"

"There's one like that on Earth as well. But we say 'Home is where the heart is.'"

He held my gaze, and I swallowed. Was he implying something about us? No. We couldn't be together. It did no good for either of us to imagine, because it was

71

never going to happen. His hand found mine again, and he squeezed it. How could such an innocent gesture be so sensual?

My heart beat faster, and I could hear the blood pounding in my ears. I pressed my legs together as a bolt of pure lust shot through my sex.

"Two people can make a home wherever they are." His voice was low and rough, and his green eyes in the light of the two moons were mesmerizing.

But I couldn't afford to be drawn in. Wasn't I smarter than that? I smiled softly and gently pulled my hand away. "I guess I don't miss all the mess." It was hard to ignore whatever had happened between us a second ago, but I was trying. "Earth is an ugly planet now. That's why I don't want to go back there."

"Sophie," he started, and I wondered briefly what he was going to say. But his computer flashed through his jacket. "It's Mother." His eyebrows drew together. "Morda's here."

"You better go welcome her." My smile became stiff and forced. "You should get to know each other better before you're joined for all eternity."

"Sophie, that's not funny. I'm not going without you. When you meet her, you'll see why."

"I'm not your buffer." Now I was beginning to feel irritated.

"Of course you are," he said, pulling me up to a standing position and opening the railing of my hover pad. "Why else would you have come all the way across the galaxy, if it wasn't to protect me from my fiancée?"

I snorted. But that impudent grin had me, and I couldn't say no to him. I climbed back onto my disc, forgetting to be nervous. "I'll just meet her and then drift away." A half-smile played on my lips. "Literally."

He laughed. "Sophie, what am I going to do without you?"

Just like that, the tension arose between us again.

"You'll be happy with your fabulous new wife. She's not me, of course. But everything will work out for you."

He gave me a rueful smile and shook his head. Pressing down on his railing, he guided his hover pad down. I watched him go, beginning to realize my heart was longing for something it could never have.

CHAPTER 6

KHELLEN

My mind was spinning around. I had felt confused about my feelings ever since I saw Sophie on the beach, but whatever had happened between Sophie and me on the cloud floaters had thrown me for a loop. I had never felt like that before, and I didn't know what to make of it. The moment I had shared with Sophie made me realize that something might be wrong with marrying Morda, and I wasn't sure if I could go through with it.

After returning our discs, Sophie and I made our way to where my parents stood with Morda and her family. Sophie stood beside me, and I had an uncomfortable feeling as I stood between the two women. On the clouds, she had insinuated that it was a bad idea to entertain hopes of our relationship ever being anything more than friendship.

I wasn't sure how she felt about me, but I knew her thoughts on marriage. Single for Life was her life. She had explicitly said so. And she certainly didn't need a man in her life.

That was good, wasn't it? It made everything simple. I was going to be marrying Morda. Sophie was merely visiting and then going home to a life of martyrdom.

Somehow it didn't feel simple at all.

Mother made introductions all around, and Morda's parents left after a couple of minutes of small talk to find some refreshments. The superficial conversation died down to a whisper until the four of us stood silently looking at each other. Uncomfortable didn't begin to describe the atmosphere.

Morda wore a red dress that ended mid-thigh and showed a fair amount of cleavage. She had pulled her hair into a little bun — perhaps an attempt at elegance — but she still looked like a child. I remembered how aroused I had been by her and couldn't understand why. The image of Sophie had replaced any attraction I had for any other woman.

"So, Morda," Sophie began, and she shifted slightly away from me. I belatedly realized we had been standing together on one side of the circle as if we were with each other. "What do you do for a living?"

I turned towards Morda, moving closer and making it look like we belonged together. I reminded myself that Morda and I were a couple.

"I'm a systems analyst," she said. "I work for Jorgencorp, one of the biggest companies on Biyaha. Have you heard of it?"

My stomach began to tie itself into knots. I felt embarrassed. Sophie was nodding with a curious expression on her face, but she was avoiding eye contact with me. Morda was trying to impress someone. My mother or Sophie, I didn't know who. I was embarrassed for her, even if she didn't seem worried about anything.

Morda continued to brag about her job until my mother stepped in, bringing the discussion around to the wedding, which she must have considered a neutral topic. Or maybe she wanted to remind us all who I was going to marry. It's not like any of us were going to forget it. The wedding was one of the worst topics she could have introduced, considering the way I felt.

"Has Khellen told you about what we're planning, Sophie?" Morda gushed, taking my hand. I felt like wrenching it out of her grip.

Sophie's smile looked false, and there was a spark of something in her eyes that I couldn't interpret. "Not yet. I got in only this morning, and we haven't had much time to catch up."

My mind moved rapidly through a series of images of Sophie since she had arrived. Sophie on the beach, throwing herself into my arms. Sophie meeting my mother. Sophie on The Boat wearing that skimpy bikini. Sophie a few minutes ago in her maddeningly sexy dress telling me in no uncertain terms that we had no business thinking about anything other than friendship. Sophie trying to ignore my uncouth fiancée's disturbing lack of social grace. Had she only been here one day? It seemed like I hadn't existed before she arrived.

"Right, Khellen? Won't it be romantic?" Morda was saying something, and I popped back into reality with a nasty shock. I had no idea what they were talking about.

"Yes?"

Sophie took pity on me, though my mother was giving me the evil eye. "Getting married on The Boat is an excellent idea, Morda. I'm sure Khellen loves it. Right, Khellen?" She gave me a frown. I knew I needed to pay attention because she wouldn't bail me out again.

"Getting married on The Boat? I don't remember deciding that." I felt my lips tense, and Morda tilted her head like a little bird.

"It was yesterday, when we met to finalize some of the plans. Your mother suggested it, and you agreed."

I vaguely remember nodding my head and saying yes to whatever they asked me. I thought I would have remembered if they mentioned The Boat, though. I raised my eyebrow at my mother.

"Maybe you were out of the room when we discussed it," she conceded. I would not have agreed to have the wedding on The Boat. It was where my father and I had spent hours together before he died. It was a private place, and I didn't want to desecrate it by having it be a place I would join with a woman I didn't love.

"We haven't decided anything yet," I said to Sophie. "It's still quite a few days away. The yard would do just as well, wouldn't it, Mother?" I tried to make my tone intimidating.

"I suppose it would be nice."

"Oh, yes, the yard! Could we have it set up like this?" Morda asked, stepping closer to me and putting her arm around my waist. I didn't like her touching me, at all. "It looks lovely with all the lights."

This arrangement would be entirely inappropriate for a traditional wedding, which was what my mother desired and what Morda agreed to. I started questioning her judgment.

That was enough wedding talk for me, so I changed the subject to the only thing I could think of. "Morda, when are you leaving for your trip?" My fingers itched to remove her arm from my waist.

"I thought maybe I shouldn't go." She gazed up at me with big eyes. "I would miss you too much."

I didn't believe for a second that she had any feelings for me. Morda was overacting to impress my mother, encouraging Mom to like her. She was the same person who had cut off my efforts to get to know her and insisted that our marriage would be a business deal. And then, if I recalled correctly, she put her hand in my pants. Who was she trying to kid?

I felt nauseous at the thought that she might not go. Right now was my only time with Sophie before the marriage and before she returned to Earth. I might never see her again in the flesh. And if I did, what difference would it make? I would be married, and she would still be single — forever — and probably running the organization. I didn't want Morda to come between us. Not yet. Not until we were officially married.

"Isn't it a business trip?" I asked. I knew she liked to look more important than she was. "You can't possibly skip it, can you? It might cost you your job."

Morda thought about what I said. "You might have a point. I really should go. I guess it doesn't matter. Once we're married, we'll have plenty of time to get to know each other. Our whole lives, right?"

She lifted her chin to look up at me, and I tried to smile at her, though I didn't think I was very convincing.

"Right." Even I could hear the tension in my voice.

"Where is it that you're going?" My mother stepped in, joining the conversation.

"I'm going to Marka," Morda said. "I hope everything goes all right. There's talk of solar storms, but it's too late to change the conference dates." She gave my mother an apologetic smile.

"Oh, I heard about those storms. They've been canceling shuttle flights right and left," my mother said, sounding genuinely concerned.

"I'm sure I'll be back in time, Fiona."

My mother smiled. "Of course you will. Everything will work out."

The conversation shifted to other topics, and I excused myself to get a much-needed drink. When I returned, I saw my mother and Morda on the fourth level, playing a game. I waved to them and went to find Sophie.

* * *

SOPHIE

After escaping Khellen's mother and fiancée, I had found my way through the darkness and ended up at The Boat, illuminated by a sliver of light coming from the twin moons guarding the night sky.

I put my hands on my flushed cheeks and closed my eyes, thankful for the shadows that sheltered me. I needed to hide away from any prying gazes that I knew could see right into my traitorous heart. I was sure everyone had seen my emotions flitting across my face like the clouds moving across the moons.

I had many conflicting feelings. Irritation at Khellen for putting me in such an awkward situation. Frustration with his mother for giving me the cold shoulder even when I knew she wasn't completely unreasonable. Disappointment and sorrow for myself and my unexpected feelings for Khellen.

After the uncomfortable conversation with Khellen's mother and his bride-to-be, I was forced to come to a painful conclusion about myself. I was jealous of Morda. Morda had Khellen, and I wanted him. It was that simple. I covered my face with my hands.

Why had I come here?

Why hadn't I stayed home, satisfied with our long-distance friendship? Why hadn't I left well enough alone? Now it was too late to protect my heart. Everyone's feelings were entangled, and no one would escape unhurt. It was a disaster — especially for me.

Khellen still had to marry Morda. But Khellen might have some feelings for me. And I had feelings for him.

I was an idiot.

* * *

KHELLEN

I searched all over the party for Sophie, stopping in every once in a while to check on Morda and my mother, who seemed to be having a very pleasant time playing cards. But she was nowhere to be found. She wasn't in her bedroom or on any of the levels of the party. The attendants at the hover pad distribution hadn't seen her since we had come through earlier.

Where was she?

After nearly an hour of roaming around the house, trying not to look like I was looking for someone, I gave up. Apparently, she didn't want to be found. I could respect that, but I wondered if I had done something to offend her.

I probably shouldn't have made her meet Morda in front of everyone like that. It resulted in an awkward conversation for everyone. But we had limited days together before she had to leave. I didn't want to waste any of that time. We would never get it back.

I needed a break. Heading down to The Boat to hide out for a while until I could get up the strength to go back to the party seemed like a great idea. After that, I would mingle for another hour and say good-bye to everyone. That would give me a few days away from Morda, during which I would need to prepare myself to see her every day of my life. I swallowed hard at the thought. Taking off my shoes and socks once I left the light of the party, I walked the rest of the way to the shore barefoot.

When I reached the lake, I gazed up at the twin moons. They gave me a sense of peace that I sorely needed, and I breathed deeply. I could relax for a while on the couches in the dark, take a rest, and then return to the house.

Stepping onto The Boat, I marveled at her stability. She hardly rocked when I set foot on her. I padded back toward the couches and chairs in the darkness under the canopy. As I approached, a shadow stood up as the moons went behind a cloud.

Someone was on The Boat. Was it someone from the party? Maybe someone wanted to go for a moonlight cruise or have a private party on my boat. This was my place. How dare they invade my sanctuary?

I threw myself at the intruder and tackled him to the ground. He let out a groan and lay still. Had I knocked him out? My arms were wrapped around the stranger, and I slowly became aware that the trespasser was disconcertingly soft, particularly in the chest region.

I had protected The Boat from a woman. Great.

"Khellen?" Sophie's voice came out of the darkness to me, and there was such longing in it that all the breath went out of my lungs.

The light from the moons came back, and Sophie looked up at me with an intimate expression on her face. I didn't move. I knew I wanted to kiss her, but I wasn't sure if she wanted to kiss me.

My body was on fire. She squirmed under me, which only increased my desire. Her eyes drifted to my lips and back up to my eyes. Her breathing was short and quick, either because I was crushing her or because she was as turned on as I was. I took some of my weight on my forearms and looked down at her lips, which looked red, full, and soft in the moonlight. Her breasts pressed against me, and I could feel my heart beating like a drum against them.

I hesitated only a moment longer. I might never get another chance like this. I dipped my head and pressed my lips to hers. The world exploded and shards of passion went flying through my chest. All my blood seemed to rush to my cock as she made a small sound in the back of her throat and opened her mouth. My tongue reached out and touched hers, sending bursts of lust through my body. I felt myself heating up as if I had a fever. Soon, our mouths were fucking. I thrust my tongue in and out of her lips, and she moaned again, arching her hips up against my hardness.

My hands became tangled in her hair, and she wrapped her arms around my back, pulling me as close as she could. Our bodies were melded together — close, but not close enough. I needed to be skin-to-skin and buried deep inside her.

I don't know what would have happened if I hadn't heard my mother's voice calling me.

"Khellen!" Her voice was faint but clear. She had probably guessed I was hiding out on The Boat. My mother knew me well.

Sophie broke the kiss, gasping and struggling to get up. I got off her, and she moved away from me. Her arms crossed over her chest, which was heaving with her irregular breathing. I gazed at her, looking both disheveled and unbelievably beautiful in the moonlight.

It wasn't fair that I couldn't hold her. How could something that felt like this be wrong? It didn't make any sense. Kissing Sophie had been an exquisite torture because I wanted to do more with her, yet I understood that I never would. But my body wouldn't soon forget the feeling of her moving beneath me.

We stared at each other, and I thought I saw my dismay and longing echoed in her eyes.

"This can't happen again."

"I know. Soph—"

"Don't call me that." Her words instantly hurt me, but when I saw the tears shining in her eyes, I knew why she was saying them. "A nickname will only make things harder, Khellen."

I nodded, swallowing my pain. "But listen, Sophie, I want to apologize for letting that get out of hand."

"We didn't do anything. Not really."

I avoided her eyes, unable to agree.

"We should go back to the house," she said, rubbing her arms with her hands as if she were cold, though the night was warm. The moons that had chased each other all night had begun to take separate courses; each would now set in a different position in the sky. It was part of their regular orbital patterns. But it made me feel empty and desolate to see them apart from each other.

"Separately," she added as if I didn't know that we shouldn't be seen together.

Without replying, I turned and headed back to the house. I rubbed my mouth, wishing I could erase the feel of her lips from mine. There was a frustrating morass of emotions in my gut that I didn't want to examine or deal with. But one thing was starting to become apparent to me.

There was no way I could marry Morda.

CHAPTER 7

SOPHIE

I sat unmoving on The Boat. My heart felt torn to shreds, and my body was a living flame of desire — no, make that unsatisfied desire. Tears rolled down my cheeks when Khellen walked away without a word. Dropping my head, I held back the sobs threatening to erupt from my throat.

Why did people want to fall in love? I didn't understand it at all. I was falling for Khellen — if I weren't already deeply in love with him. And I could never have him.

I wrapped my arms around my torso, rocking myself in an attempt to contain the agony in my heart. The pain spread, and I drew in deep gasps trying to catch my breath. Now I understood what my mother had meant about regretting my decision to commit to Single for Life. But even if I hadn't made the vow, Khellen was taken. And it didn't matter that he didn't even like her. It didn't matter that he found me attractive and surely had feelings for me. None of that mattered because he had just given his word and he needed to keep it. Just as I had sworn a vow and couldn't break it. There was no way we could ever be together. I would have to accept our decisions.

* * *

After ten minutes, I returned to the party, hoping I didn't look like a mess. I had washed my face in the lake. The French twist was beyond repair, so I had pulled it apart and used my fingers to rearrange my hair. After straightening my dress and holding my head up high, I started walking back toward the house.

As I emerged from the darkness, I saw Khellen's mother staring at me, outrage evident on her face. She was a woman; of course she knew what happened when no one was watching. If I looked as disheveled as I thought I did, she probably thought we had done more than kiss each other. No doubt my forlorn look told her everything she needed to know about my feelings for Khellen.

I drew myself up to my full height and fixed a pleasant expression on my face, giving her a nod and heading for the side of the house. I made a beeline straight up to my room, not stopping to talk to anyone. When I got there, I pulled the dress off carelessly and threw it over a chair. Stripping off my underclothes, I slunk into the shower and turned it on as hot as I could stand it. I let the hot water run over my head and down my face, washing away the tears that I couldn't hold back any longer. Finally, the sobs came, torn from deep inside me. I cried until my stomach muscles were sore and my eyes burned. I had nothing left in me. Finally, I let the warm water soothe and comfort me.

After the shower, I set my BioScan on the floor and let it do its magic. It was a habit, and I was merely going through the motions. I checked the app for any abnormalities other than stress hormones but saw nothing worrisome. It seemed impossible that feeling this bad had no physical effects.

I felt like I had been through the wringer. Had I only arrived in the morning? So much had happened that it didn't seem possible. Could someone fall in love this fast? I had heard of love at first sight and read about it in books. I even had a friend from school who had met her husband, moved in with him a couple of weeks later, and was pregnant within a month. They bought a house, had a baby, and married all in less than a year. And they were still together! They seemed like they would last forever. I had never seen such a happy couple. And I had never imagined it could happen to me, a person who had vowed never to marry or have children. No wonder Single for Life marketed to people in their teens. Only someone who had never been in love would make such a reckless vow.

At this point, if Khellen asked me to marry him, I don't know what I would say. I knew what I ought to say, but I wasn't sure I could refuse him. If he wanted to have sex, unprotected sex, I don't know if I would turn him down. Unprotected sex was the only kind we could legally have on Biyaha, where it was a crime to use contraceptives. I certainly hadn't brought any with me because sex with anything wasn't on the agenda when I planned the trip.

I shivered and my hips bucked at the thought of fucking Khellen. My boyfriend and I had always been safe, and the idea of having nothing between Khellen and me was maddening.

I couldn't believe I was contemplating having unprotected sex. Who had I become in the space of a day? How had everything in my world been turned upside down by one man? And how was I going to live my life without him?

* * *

KHELLEN

I paced back and forth in my old bedroom. It was past midnight. The party had been over for a long time. I hadn't seen Sophie after leaving her on The Boat, but I had thought of nothing else since. I had chatted absentmindedly with Morda and her parents, but they left early so she could get ready for her business trip. Of course, I couldn't break up with her at the party. A video call would have to do. It was almost as good as face-to-face communication, and there wasn't time for anything else.

As soon as I returned to my room, I had tried to contact Morda to call off the engagement. She was unreachable. I had been so desperate that I even called her mother. It turned out that Morda had caught her flight, a red-eye off the planet leaving an hour before I started trying to reach her. She wouldn't be back until the night before the wedding. I hadn't realized she was going right away. When I had asked for a contact number, her mother explained that the trip was a team retreat, and they weren't taking any calls.

She hadn't wanted to listen when I told her it was an emergency, but she eventually relented and gave me the contact information for Morda's supervisor. I was left staring at the number on my comm unit. No matter how badly I wanted to be free of Morda, I wasn't going to dump her through her boss.

I sat on my bed with my head in a mess. I didn't even want to think about my tangled emotions. It hurt too much. The only thing I knew was that my marriage to Morda was ill-advised, considering my feelings for Sophie.

I thought I had been in love before, but it was a slight stirring in my soul compared to the thunderstorm of feelings I had for Sophie. If I wasn't in love, I didn't know what was happening to me. My behavior over the past twenty-four hours had been irrational and so far from normal that I hardly recognized myself.

It took another hour of pacing before I was calm enough to take a shower, get on my pajamas, and go to sleep. My dreams were all of Sophie being close to me but just out of reach. Time after time, I couldn't catch her. Finally, I woke up to the silver-green light of dawn, feeling even more exhausted than when I went to bed. I decided to go for my morning swim. Perhaps returning to a routine would help me forget about yesterday's madness.

Swimming did give me a temporary feeling of peacefulness. But when I went back to the house and thought about Sophie sleeping peacefully somewhere inside, I became frustrated all over again. Was I going to follow my head or my heart?

Before I had to make a decision, my computer flashed, and I glanced at the screen. It was a message from Morda. I considered deleting it before I read what she had to say but ignored the childish urge. I swiped it open, wondering what she wanted to discuss. Hadn't we just seen each other? As I read further, I appreciated that I hadn't deleted it. The feeling of relief was so strong that I had to sit down on the bed because my legs wouldn't support me.

Morda had landed safely on Marka. But immediately after her arrival, the intensity of the solar storms required them to ground all the spaceflights. Communications on the planet were intermittent, and the storms were ongoing. She wouldn't be able to return to Biyaha for at least another week, maybe more. That meant that she wouldn't return in time to marry before my birthday. She apologized but said I would have to find someone else.

I grinned at my incredible luck. But now I needed to find someone to marry again. This time, I knew the right girl, and nothing could go wrong.

* * *

I snuck up the back stairway to avoid running into my mother. I couldn't face her today, not yet. Not until after I talked with Sophie. I didn't know what I was going to say, but I had to fix the fiasco on The Boat. I stood outside her door for a few minutes feeling like a boy working up the nerve to talk to his crush.

Finally, I made myself knock on the door. I wasn't twelve years old. There was no answer, but I heard someone moving around in the room.

"Sophie?" I called through the door. "I need to talk to you, please."

There was no response.

"I'll only be a minute. Will you please open the—"

The door opened abruptly, and Sophie stood in front of me looking as terrible as I felt. Her eyes looked puffy. Her hair in a messy braid. And she was wearing sweatpants and a T-shirt that was so big on her that it was falling off one bare shoulder.

She still looked beautiful to me. I pulled my gaze away from the sight of her skin.

"Can I come in for a minute?"

"I don't think that's a good idea." Her voice was tight, her face unhappy.

"Then come walk with me. Please, Sophie. We need to talk. It's important."

"Fine." She stepped out the doorway and pulled it closed behind her.

We went down the back stairs and out the side door. We followed a path to a boardwalk that ran the length of the lake on the far side, away from our house. A person could walk for hours beside the lake undisturbed if they wanted to. It was perfect.

Neither one of us said anything. I was trying to figure out the right words. I wasn't sure why Sophie was quiet, but she wasn't pleased with me, and I didn't blame her.

"First of all, I want to apologize for last night," I said, not knowing where else to begin.

"Apologize." She sounded pissed, and I wondered what I had done wrong already.

"Yes, apologize. Keep your voice down, Sophie. Sound carries across the water."

"For what, exactly?" She spoke barely above a whisper, her bearing stiff and upset.

"For letting things get out of hand."

"Is that what you call what happened last night? A mistake?"

"I'm not apologizing for kissing you if that's what you mean."

Her steps slowed, and she started to look relaxed, but her expression was still wary. "Then what are you apologizing for?"

"For letting it go past a kiss into something more than a kiss, I suppose. It was wrong because I know your beliefs. I shouldn't have let things go that far. If my mother hadn't interrupted, I'm not sure what would have happened."

Her eyes slid away from mine. We both knew what would have happened if my mother hadn't called me.

"You know, we didn't do anything unforgivable." She said something similar last night as she looked away from me out across the lake.

"Come on. We need to talk in private, where we won't be overheard." Part of me wanted to reach out and take her hand. I didn't think she would welcome me touching her right now.

"I agree."

"Good. I know a place." I led her off the boardwalk and back to my house.

"Grab your suit and we'll go to the island."

"Have you forgotten something? I can't swim, Khellen."

"Just wear the life band and you'll be fine."

"Why can't we take The Boat?"

"Well, its absence will be noticeable, for one thing." Then I responded with a more practical answer. "It's hot. And you wanted to spend time in the water, right? We can talk undisturbed while on the island. Meet me down by the water in your swimsuit in five minutes."

* * *

It didn't take us long to cross to the isle. She may not have swum before, but Sophie was a natural athlete and

94

soon figured out the stroke I used. We reached the island in about ten minutes. It was slower than my usual speed but pretty good for someone without any experience.

We took a steep path off the beach that emerged onto a ledge about four feet deep and ten feet long. When the ridge ended, the cliff fell away dropping down about twenty feet to the forest below. From up here we could see the beach and the lake in the distance. My mother's house was barely visible, the roof peeking through the purple treetops. Sophie came out behind me a second later and sucked in her breath.

"You should have taken me here first." Her voice was soft. We stood side by side admiring the view. The purple forest stretched away, dotted with blue lakes and isolated houses. "It's beautiful."

I turned to look at her and said the first thing that popped into my head. "So are you."

Even without preparing her face, after a night of what had been a restless sleep, with dark circles under her eyes and baggy clothes — even then, she looked good to me. She was the most gorgeous woman I had ever seen.

It looked like she didn't even hear me.

"Marry me, Sophie." My words surprised me even though they had been at the back of my mind ever since I brought her here.

She continued to stare at the view. "Don't be ridiculous. You're engaged to Morda, and I'm single for life."

"Morda can't return to the planet in time. Solar storms delayed her. She won't be here before my birthday."

She stared at me. "Khellen, this isn't a good idea."

"Please," I begged, taking her hands. "I need you."

She appeared to be unmoved, so I brought out the arguments I had prepared on our way here. "It will be a marriage of convenience. You'd be doing it to help me out."

"Wow, that sounds terrific." I wondered if I detected the hint of disappointment in her eyes. "I'd love to participate in a business arrangement on my vacation, but my life on Earth would be ruined. I would lose my job and credibility in the organization. Everything I've worked toward would vanish."

I dropped my head, looking at the ground, trying to figure out how to change her mind. "We wouldn't have to tell anyone on Earth. Marry me for a year. We'll keep it secret. Take a leave of absence. At the end of the year, we get divorced. I don't disappear forever, you go back to your life, and no one is the wiser."

I watched as her face went blank. "It would be a marriage of convenience? A marriage in name only?"

"Yes," I said, never taking my eyes away from hers. "What else could it be?"

She blinked, her face a steely mask that gave nothing away. "Of course, what else?" she repeated, a faraway look in her eye. And even though I had no right to expect anything, I felt like she had taken my heart out and stomped on it. "Are you sure no one would find out?"

We began to work out the details.

"My mother works in the vital statistics division, remember? We get married, and she'll enter the information into the system. No one will have to know. Can you get a leave of absence?"

"I think so. I'm friends with my boss, Nora, so I should be able to. She won't be happy when I don't start my new position right away, but the person I'm replacing wanted to ease into retirement gradually, letting me take on more and more responsibility until she was ready to leave. She'll just have to start transferring her load a year later than she planned."

"Good. You can be my mail order bride." I tried to lighten the mood with a joke. She glared at me, but I couldn't seem to stop talking. "In the old days when the Great Race was moving out into the galaxy, there were more men than women on the colonization planets. They would message back and forth with a woman and then she would—"

"I know, Khellen." She interrupted me, her tone scathing.

"It was only a joke, Sophie. You know, because we never met in person before yesterday, and we've been corresponding."

"I said I got the joke, Khellen." Her eyes traveled over the incredible vista that lay before us, but I had a feeling she wasn't seeing it anymore.

"Sophie?" She didn't look at me. "What do you say? Will you marry me?"

When she finally turned to meet my eye, there was nothing but sad resignation on her face. "Sure," she said, her eyes empty. "Why not? To help you out. Because we're friends."

At that moment, I felt we were as far from friends as two people could be.

CHAPTER 8

SOPHIE

How could I have been so clueless? Khellen wasn't interested in me. Sure, he wanted me physically. We had chemistry together, but he didn't care about me as anything other than a friend. He needed me to marry him because he didn't want to be taken by his government. If our positions were reversed, I'm sure I would have asked him to assist me as well.

The sick feeling in my stomach was because I thought he might have the same feelings for me that I had for him. I had believed that we might be falling in love. Lust was not the same as love, and I had gotten the two mixed up. I was going to pay because I cared about Khellen more than he cared about me. It was a recipe for a broken heart.

The hours passed in a blur as Khellen and his mother made the arrangements. Everything would be done in complete secrecy to protect me.

I contacted Nora and told her that my friend needed me on Biyaha. He was going through a hard time, and I planned to stay if she would approve a one-year leave of absence. She was reluctant to grant my request, but I told her that if she denied my request, I would have to reassess my future with the organization. That changed her tune quickly. Single for Life had a hard time recruiting staff, so once they found a good employee, they did their best to keep them. Nora sent the paperwork immediately.

The next step was going to the temple to get married in the evening. We wore ordinary clothes in order not to arouse suspicions. Khellen's mother would be the witness. There would be no fanfare. No guests. Nothing but a contract between two people. It seemed appropriate. I was having a hard time balancing the desires of my heart with the knowledge in my head. Empty eyes stared back at me from the mirror. How had my life gotten so turned around in such a short time?

* * *

The three of us rushed down the beaten path to the temple and entered through a side door.

"Welcome," said the priest. "Do you have the donation, Fiona?"

Khellen's mother held out an envelope. His mother had offered an enormous contribution to the temple, securing the priest's silence on the matter.

The middle-aged man smiled and tucked the envelope beneath his green robes. With a flourish of his hand, he indicated that we should stand by the altar. Khellen and I moved into position facing the priest. His mother sat in a pew at the front. I didn't hear anything until the priest told us to join hands. Khellen had to reach out and take mine because I hadn't offered them. If the priest noticed any coldness between us, he gave no indication of anything unusual.

"Embrace," the priest intoned, and Khellen pulled me into his arms. His warmth felt good and bad at the same time. I knew he was only doing it because he had to, not because he wanted to.

I couldn't resist asking a question. "How can you trust me to make a vow to you when I'll be breaking another promise?"

I could tell that he had been about to release me, but didn't after I spoke. I felt his breath on my ear and barely repressed a shiver. "You made a promise to stay single on Earth, Sophie. You're not on Earth anymore."

My mind reeled as he let me go. He was right. Was I technically breaking my vow at all? Perhaps it had been written that way on purpose. The commitment didn't matter if you weren't living on Earth. Most planets didn't have an overpopulation problem. For the first time, I began to feel better.

Khellen smiled as the light dawned on me and I let him take my hands again.

"Do you, Khellen John Lynch swear to take Sophie Enya McCallistair for your lawful wife, to have and to hold from this day forward, for better, for worse, for richer, for poorer, in sickness and health, until death do you part?"

Khellen gazed directly into my eyes, and I saw nothing but the truth as he spoke. "I do."

Two words caused my bad feelings to return. I knew it was a lie. I didn't blame him for it; I only wished we could have married under different circumstances.

"Do you, Sophie Enya McCallistair, take Khellen John Lynch for your lawful husband, to have and to hold from this day forward, for better, for worse, for richer, for poorer, in sickness and health, until death do you part?"

I held his gaze, knowing he thought I was only saying it for a show, too. But I meant it. "I do."

The priest smiled kindly. "Do you have the bands?" I watched as Khellen pulled out two thin silver bands that gave off a rainbow gleam when he turned them in the light. "Put one on Sophie," the priest instructed. Khellen slid the band up my left arm, almost to the elbow. When it became tight, I watched it meld into my skin, leaving a bright rainbow circling my arm that seemed like it was part of me. It would be difficult to remove. "Now repeat after me."

Khellen looked nervous but spoke in a firm voice, repeating everything the priest said. "I, Khellen John Lynch, swear by this band that I choose you, Sophie Enya McCallistair above all others, to be my wife. I offer this ring as a token of our love and faithfulness and with it I join my life to yours. As this ring has no end, neither shall my love for you."

I slid Khellen's band onto his arm, and when I glanced up, he was looking at me with an unreadable expression. I repeated the words after the priest. He said we could seal our vows with a kiss.

I nervously waited as Khellen leaned in to press his lips to mine. It started out chaste and then he put his arms around me and kissed me until I couldn't remember my name, which was just as well because I was about to change it.

When he pulled away, my legs were rubbery, and my mind was blank. His eyes looked intense, and if we had been alone, I would have worried about my vow to remain barren. Just because I was on another planet didn't mean I wanted to get pregnant.

I told myself I was not going to have sex with Khellen. Khellen's mother approached, gave us each a peck on the cheek, and offered congratulations, as did the priest. I smiled and nodded. I don't remember saying anything. Soon Khellen took my hand and led me out of the temple as if he knew my head was in a muddle.

As we walked outside, he released me in case anyone was watching us. To my surprise, my hand felt cold and empty without his. We followed a few feet behind his mother. He leaned towards me and whispered. "The priest doesn't do the certificates; we have to go to the government office where Mom works. She'll complete the certification process for us."

"Certificates?" I hissed. "They'll be embedded in our forearms, where everyone can see them. And what about these bands? They are obvious, too. Our marriage is supposed to be a secret, Khellen."

"We took care of that. We brought cream that will conceal imprints in the skin. It will cover both the certificate and the bands."

"Are you sure?" I was starting to panic. For a brief moment, I had entertained the idea that I might make a new life for myself with Khellen. Now that he had proved the dream was gone, my work was all I had left. I wasn't going to lose that for him.

"I'm sure, Mrs. Lynch," he said, that last part under his breath. I felt a sizzling thrill as I realized that I was his wife now, whether he loved me or not. Even though I considered myself to be a modern woman, I liked having his name now. I was his, and by extension, he was mine. Morda couldn't have him now. No one else could.

If only I had the love that was supposed to go along with this arrangement. I sighed slowly, attracting his attention. His mother had pulled ahead and was practically running as if she were nervous.

"Why the sigh, Mrs. Lynch?"

"You don't have to call me that. Don't pretend this is something it's not."

My words deflated him slightly. I regretted my response for an instant until I remembered that he didn't love me. "What if I like calling you by that name?" he asked.

"Don't call me that even if you like to. It's supposed to be a secret. Let's keep it." I tried to remind him gently. "I'm doing you a favor, but I don't want it to ruin my life."

The happiness I saw in his eyes before was gone, and I wondered why I was picking a fight. Did I want to hurt him as much as he had hurt me? "I won't let marrying me ruin your life," he said, and his eyes became emotionless. "I promise."

"Good," I said. He held the door open for me, and I walked into the government building. "I'll hold you to that."

It was close to the end of the workday. The wedding was timed this way to avoid unnecessary complications. She was already sitting at her desk when we went in, with only an imprinting machine and a bottle of white liquid on her otherwise clean desk.

"Let's get right to it. The marriage certificate imprint, as you know, is the same as a birth certificate. It can't come off without using a laser." She was consummate in her role as civil servant. "Please swab your mouths to provide a DNA sample and bare your left forearms for the imprint."

She inserted the swabs into the device and began entering data about the marriage. I could see the photo from the priest displayed on the screen as she waited for the machine to finish processing the information. I flipped my left forearm over, running my finger across the shiny silver band about a quarter-inch thick. Rainbows played across the metal whenever the light hit it.

"It looks good on you," Khellen whispered. He sat with his left forearm lying on his lap, facing up. The band sparkled in the light. Of course, everything looked good on him. He was so handsome that he would make a paper bag look fantastic. I imagined that he would look good wearing nothing but the band, as well.

"Hold your arm up." His mother spoke to me as if I weren't her daughter-in-law, but an annoying citizen she wanted to get out of her office as quickly as possible. Khellen glared at her but didn't say anything.

I held my forearm up, and she pressed the device against my arm. It felt warm for a moment and then I felt nothing. She pulled it away, moving to Khellen to tag him as well.

I examined my arm. When I turned it to the light, I could see data about the marriage was there as well as a photo of Khellen and me at the ceremony. At the bottom, I could see a DNA signature that made the certificates impossible to forge. Looking at the license and the band next to it, I felt a heavy weight in my heart. Marriage was supposed to be forever, and we were playing with it.

"Now for the most complicated part of this operation - covering it up," his mother said, a disgruntled look on her face. "The compound is a little overwhelming and can obscure an imprint in the skin. That means it's difficult to remove. When the time comes, you can go to a doctor, who will use a laser and anesthetic to get it off."

"Are you sure that no one will be able to see the certificates or the bands?" I needed to be certain.

His mother pressed her lips together and looked furious, but she managed to answer politely. "No one will see anything. This stuff isn't cheap, you know."

"I can pay you back," I said quickly.

"I didn't tell you to get my credits. We can afford it. I want you to know it's a quality product that you don't need to worry about. Now hold out your arm again and don't move."

I held still while she painted over the band first, then the certificate. It dried instantly, and my arm looked like nothing had happened today. Even though this was what I wanted, I felt a sense of loss as the proof of our wedding vanished from existence. It was all a sham, anyway. I had no right to look like his wife with these markings. I noticed a corner of the concealing patch sticking up and scraped my nail across it. It appeared to be a piece of dried skin.

"Don't pick at it," Khellen's mother said sharply. "It can loosen if you tug on it hard enough, and it's painful for you if you try to pull it off. Remember - anesthetic."

I shuddered, haunted by a mental picture of tearing the compound off. I wondered if my flesh would come off with it.

"Okay," I said, tucking my arm against my side to stop myself from picking at it again.

I glanced over at Khellen, whose face was expressionless as his mother painted over his band and certificate, hiding our union from everyone. Only the three of us and the priest knew what had happened.

It was turning out to be quite a marriage.

* * *

KHELLEN

I had conflicted feelings about the wedding. It had been sweet torment as I swore to love Sophie till death do us part, all the while knowing that she was only going to be married to me for a year, and only because she was helping out a friend.

When the priest told me to kiss her and seal our vows, I had been planning to give her a peck on the lips. I didn't intend to torture myself by kissing her the way I wanted. But once my lips were on hers, I lost control of myself, pulling her close and kissing her passionately, forgetting that we weren't alone. When I let her go, she looked dazed. At least we were physically compatible, even if we were only friends with benefits to her.

As much as I wanted to make love to Sophie, I knew it would be a rash decision. It would be painful to possess her while knowing I would have to say goodbye to her forever in a year. I knew I would have to work to keep my hands off her, but it would be worth it. I didn't want to touch her and have a haunting memory replayed in my mind forever as she went about her life on Earth, saving her people from themselves.

When my mother finished, I stared at my bare arm, grateful that Sophie had saved me, but wondering what might have been. If she had stayed across the galaxy, I would never have fallen in love with her and had my heart disturbed. But when I studied her across the room, observing her beauty and intelligence I had to admit I was lucky. Spending the next year with her was going to be bittersweet knowing she would leave me at the end. But I would have her for that time, and she would be mine.

When she returned to Earth, at least she wouldn't be going back there for another man. I wondered if she would remember me, a galaxy away, as she sat in her office at Single for Life.

"We're finished," my mother said. "Let's get out of here."

"Aren't you going to enter it into the system?" I asked. "You know, the whole reason why we're getting married in the first place?"

She shook her head and pointed to the clock. "I can't anymore. Look." We watched the clock go past the hour. "We timed it almost perfectly, but now it's after hours, and it would look strange in the logs. I'm a government worker. We don't do anything extra. If there's any work left when the day ends, it gets pushed to tomorrow."

"Why didn't you do it earlier?" I asked.

"I couldn't. I needed the numbers from the certificates. And then they needed to be covered immediately." She nodded in Sophie's direction. I hoped she calmed down soon. Her anxiety was contagious. "Let's get going and we'll talk about our options at home," she said, pulling on her coat. "We have about eleven hours before they come to arrest you, Khellen."

CHAPTER 9

KHELLEN

"Both of you have to go to the island." My mother made her announcement when we were all settled in the living room, each holding a cup of tea. I could have done with something stronger, but my mother's solution to stress was always tea.

"Why would we do that?" I didn't understand what she was thinking.

Sophie looked back and forth between the two of us, trying to follow the conversation.

"Do you have another solution, Khellen?"

I racked my brain but came up with nothing.

"It's remote. It has a place to sleep. They won't be able to find you tomorrow when they come looking for you. The servants will tell them what I say. You'll be on a two-day trip to Evador."

"They'll figure it out."

"Eventually. But it will take time. While they're delayed, I'll enter the marriage into the system, and your name will disappear from their list. They'll assume it was a mistake or a delay. That kind of thing happens all the time. They won't think anything of it and move on to the next poor soul."

"It sounds risky," Sophie said.

"Everything we're doing is risky," Mom answered, giving Sophie a venomous glare. "But it's Khellen's choice, so I'm making it as safe as I can. What else would you like me to do?"

I rose and went over to my mother, crouching down beside her and putting my hand over hers. "We understand what you're putting on the line, Mom, and we appreciate it. We'll go to the island. It won't be a problem."

She pressed her lips together, somewhat mollified.

"You'll message me when it's safe to come back?"

"Of course."

"Pack some things, Sophie, and let's go. The sooner we've hidden away, the better. Thanks again, Mom," I said, kissing her on the cheek.

She hugged me. Sophie stood up and headed for her room, taking her tea with her. As soon as she was gone, my mother tugged on my sleeve and pulled me down to face her.

"Don't do anything stupid with her, Khellen."

"What do you mean?" I matched her unpleasant tone.

"You know what I mean. If this is only temporary because she wants to divorce you in a year and go back to her singles club, then don't make things more complicated."

"What sort of complication do you mean, Mother?"

"Don't play dumb. Just don't knock the girl up."

I opened my mouth in outrage, but she wasn't finished yet.

"Believe me. You'll regret it later when she takes your child back to Earth, and we never see either one of them again."

"This is not an appropriate conversation between a parent and her son." I felt mortified.

"Use your head. That's all I'm saying," she warned.

"I don't think you need to worry about anything. Sophie is doing me a favor." I didn't want to sound ungrateful, but I couldn't seem to keep my cool. "She's helping me out, but you don't need to worry about anything else happening."

My mother snorted and shook her head at me. "Don't be an idiot. I saw that girl when she came back from your interlude on The Boat. And I've caught some of the glances you give each other that nearly set the house on fire."

I glared at her. "I'm not sure what you mean."

"Don't tell me there's nothing between the two of you. I may be old, but I'm not that old." She folded her hands primly in her lap.

My mother had never talked to me like this before.

"Do you need me to spell it out for you? You say she's marrying you to help you out and then divorcing you, but she looks like a lovesick girl who's been tossed aside." She patted my hand. "You're a catch, especially for someone from Earth. I think she's in love with you."

"Of all the ridiculous things you've just said, Mother, that's got to be the most outrageous."

"You don't have to believe me. But I can see you've fallen for her, too. I don't know why you would get married, then pretend you don't care about each other. But figure out what you want to do. My point is, don't fuck that girl on the island without a plan for the future. I doubt you'll take my advice, but I feel better having warned you."

I shook my head. Who knew what the morning would bring? I hoped everything would go well. But if I disappeared, I didn't want to have any regrets. "Thanks for the tip."

Unsatisfied, I left the room to find my wife.

* * *

SOPHIE

The island was bigger than I had realized. When Khellen took me there so we could speak in private on the ledge, I didn't realize I only saw a small portion of it. This time, we had swum across, pulling our gear behind us in waterproof floating bags. We didn't want The Boat moored at the island as a signal that someone was there. Besides, Khellen loved swimming and jumped at any chance to hop in the water.

Instead of taking the right-hand path that led up to the ledge as we had done the first time, we went left at the fork and made our way down a large hill. At the bottom of the slope was a guest house sitting in a level clearing.

When Khellen opened the door, I frowned. The guest house consists of one room with a double bed in the corner. There were two doors at the back, which I assumed led to a bathroom and a closet.

"I only see one bed here," I said, getting right to the point.

"I'll sleep on the couch, Sophie. Don't worry. I know this isn't really our wedding night."

The rancor in his voice matched what I felt in my heart. Did he care? Oh right, he was hoping to have sex with me. One of the perks of getting married. "It's a marriage of convenience, Khellen. Sex wasn't in the deal."

"Of course not," he said, going around and opening all the windows. "Whatever you want."

"Right." *I'm not sleeping with you, buddy. You're just using me to save yourself.* I was a little shocked at the emotion in my thoughts. Did I believe that? I knew I was attracted to him, so why was he drawing such response from me?

Was he using me? I had to admit that part of me felt resentful and used. I was doing a favor for a friend far away across the galaxy. But I didn't need to give him the cold shoulder. I watched him get out sheets and pillows from what was indeed a closet at the back of the room. He brought them to the couch and stopped when he saw me staring at him. "What?"

"I'm sorry we're fighting," I murmured, dropping my eyes. I stared at my arm where the marriage certificate ought to be. The bit of compound that still hadn't adhered properly caught my attention, and I picked at it nervously. He was silent for a moment before he came over to me.

"It's not fighting, exactly." He was standing close to me but carefully avoided touching my body.

"We're not getting along, either." I looked up to meet his eyes. "Was it easier to interact with each other before I came here?"

He got a strange look on his face. "Do you wish you hadn't come?"

"No," I said more forcefully than I meant to. "Of course not. I only wish we could act naturally with each other."

He thought about that for a minute. "Why can't we?" he asked. His voice was rough.

"I don't know." I fidgeted with my hands, feeling helpless. I didn't think I could make things go back to the way they were.

"What if, just for tonight, we pretend that everything's the way it was before, Sophie? We don't know what's going to happen tomorrow. I don't want to spend what might be our last night together, arguing over trivial things."

I felt like crying. "It's not going to be our final night," I said, taking his hands and staring into his eyes.

"Maybe not. Can we stop arguing, at least?"

I smiled. "I guess so. We can certainly try."

"And let's be honest tonight. Nothing but honesty between us." The sexual innuendo made me shiver in spite of myself.

"I can do that."

"Good," he said, letting go of my hands. "Let's get this place set up and make something to eat."

* * *

After a very late meal with great conversation and a feeling of camaraderie that felt like old times, Khellen and I went to bed. I was on the double bed in the corner, and he was on the couch. It was scorching hot.

117

I'm sure it was never this hot on Earth — not where I came from. I felt like I was melting, and there was no way I could sleep. I could hear Khellen toss and turn until he finally got up. A moment later, I felt him looming over me in the darkness. "Come on, Sophie," he said, offering me his hand.

I stared at it and then up at him. "Where are we going?"

"A place where we can cool down. We're going to roast if we stay in here any longer."

"Okay." I took his hand. He pulled me up, and I threw the covers back on the bed.

"Change in the bathroom. I'll meet you outside when you're ready."

I was intrigued. I knew he wouldn't take me to the lake because someone might see us. I put on my bikini and braided my hair behind me, getting it out of the way. I went out into the main room, dropping my pajamas on the bed and slipping on my sandals.

"Ready?" Khellen's voice came from the darkness of the trees.

"I think so. Where are we going?"

"You'll see." When I reached him, he was smiling at me with happiness in his eyes. I couldn't help but smile back. "Tonight's about you and me, Sophie. No regrets."

My heart beat faster at his words. "I don't want us to fight," I whispered, trying not to think about what tomorrow might bring.

He held out his hand, so I took it and we walked forward into the night.

* * *

With Khellen's hand in mine, I was on top of the world. He led me through the dense purple trees down a path he had used since he was a boy. When we emerged from the forest, I was stunned by the beauty. "Khellen, this is incredible."

We stood at the edge of a deep natural pool. A waterfall was across from us. The clearing was surrounded by a cliff on the right and a forest all the way around on the left. The water was clear and sparkling. I had a feeling it would be unbelievably refreshing.

Khellen handed me the life band he brought for me. I wrapped it around my neck. Then, giving me a grin, he ran and launched himself into the water, pulling his legs up into a cannonball that he knew would drench me. I waited until he came to the surface, then jumped in beside him with a big splash to pay him back.

I popped up out of the water, laughing. "What a relief from the heat."

"Want to go to the waterfall?"

"I don't know."

"You know you want to go to the waterfall, Sophie." He shot me a grin that I was powerless to refuse.

All I could think was that I never wanted this moment to end.

The pool was deep, but my life band kept me afloat and I was able to make my way over to the waterfall. We went under together and emerged on the other side. I gasped when I opened my eyes. The water of the falls had concealed a cave. There was a luminescent plant on the walls giving off a dim light and lighting up the ceiling with a rainbow of colors that moved and danced. I had never seen anything like it. It felt romantic.

"Lie on your back and float," he said. "That's the best way to watch the show."

I started floating, and the life band quickly lifted me. I still couldn't believe I was in the water. Maybe someday I would learn to swim properly. Not on Earth, however. There was no chance of learning to swim on Earth. I pushed the thought of my home planet out of my head and focused on the fairy lights. Khellen took my hand so we were connected.

After a while, we left in silence and went back through the waterfall. Khellen showed me some step-like rocks on the side of the pool by the cliff. The three ledges were broad enough to lie on and still be in the water. I took the top step, and he took the middle one. My skin was starting to wrinkle, but that was a small price to pay for the comfort of the cold water.

"Are you aware you live in paradise?" I asked, looking around at the idyllic spot.

"I wasn't until you told me about Earth." I stared up at the strange constellations and was again surprised that I didn't miss home at all. "Are you homesick yet?" he asked.

I shook my head. "Not at all."

"Have you thought that maybe it's because you were meant to stay here?" His voice was so soft that I almost couldn't hear him. My pulse began to pound, and my chest rose and fell in the light of the two moons.

"I think that's not on the list of approved topics tonight. What happened to not thinking about tomorrow?"

He made a frustrated sound, and I sat up, putting my feet down on to his step, wondering what I had done to upset him. "Is something the matter?"

"I don't know, Sophie. You make me want to break all the rules in my life."

He knelt before me and took my hands. He looked up anxiously. "No regrets," he whispered, and I leaned in toward him as if drawn by a magnet.

"No regrets," I repeated.

"Do you know what, Sophie?" His eyes looked at me, unblinking.

"What?" I breathed.

"If I don't kiss you right now, I think I will regret it for the rest of my life."

My heart rate kicked up another notch, and I saw fear in his eyes. Was he afraid I was going to reject him?

"I would regret it, too. What are you waiting for?" I put my hand on his cheek. He closed his eyes but didn't move, perhaps waiting for me to show that I meant what I said.

I gazed at his beautiful face in the moonlight. The next day he might disappear, no matter what we had done to prevent that. And if he didn't, the magic of this place would be gone, and we might be back to sniping at each other.

We had a good reason for getting married. He didn't love me. But if I could have one night with him...one night to remember for the rest of my days when I was lying in my empty bed, yearning for him...

I made a conscious decision. *Tonight, he's mine.*

I leaned down and claimed his lips. Fireworks exploded behind my eyes and electricity blasting everywhere, running straight to my core. I was going to take him.

CHAPTER 10

SOPHIE

He groaned when I spread my legs and slid off the step to straddle him where he knelt. He was hard already. His lips found mine, and it felt like our mouths were made for each other. When his tongue pressed in, I opened my mouth and felt my bikini bottom getting wet.

Maybe I could have him, just for tonight.

I slipped my arms around his neck and drew him closer, twisting my fingers through his hair. His hands roamed over the skin of my back and then dropped to cup my buttocks, pulling me tight against him. Feeling his cock only excited me more.

We kissed for a long time until he worked up enough nerve to slide his hand under my bikini top and take my breast. He squeezed and massaged it, drawing the first moan from me. Khellen broke off the kiss then. "Are you sure you want to do this, Sophie?"

"Yes." I could barely speak the word. I knew he wasn't going to stop no matter what I said.

"You know it's my first time, right?"

"Don't worry, I'll be gentle," I said, taking his face in my hands and kissing him all over. I felt him smile.

"I mean, I might not last long."

"Then let's take some of the pressure off," I whispered, moving back and freeing him from his swim shorts. He popped loose, and I couldn't help but stare. He was large, but that wasn't what gave me pause. It was the coloring.

"Sorry about that," he said, sounding embarrassed. "We're bigger than humans, and I'm told our genitals are differently colored."

Colored pink. But I didn't care what color he was as long as he fucked me.

I took him in my hand. My fingers and thumb didn't quite meet, but I was able to take a good hold and pumped. He drew in a deep breath. I worked him for a while and in about a minute he was already coming. I felt a sense of satisfaction and moved away, washing him and my hand.

"Sophie," he said, and his eyes were burning. "It's your turn."

He took my hand and led me up the steps, where he lay me down onto the soft moss beside the pool. There was no need for any more words. He covered me with his hot, hard body, and I could hardly believe this was Khellen — my pen pal, my best friend, and now my lover. I wanted to remember each moment as much as I could, storing recollections for the long lonely nights that lay ahead of me.

Pulling his lips from mine, he kissed a trail down my body. He covered my arm with hot wet kisses, all the way down to my palm and back up, stopping at my elbow. Who would have thought that the elbow could be so sensitive? But I was beginning to think every inch of my body was an erogenous zone with Khellen.

I arched my back, and his hands reached beneath me. He pulled the string of the bikini, releasing it, and drew the scrap of fabric off me, leaving my breasts bare.

"You're beautiful." He bent his head, licking and kissing around my breasts until I was writhing in pleasure, needing him to take my nipples. But he made me wait, drawing out the moment. He licked one dark pink bud, and I sucked in a sharp breath, shivering when he blew on it.

I needed him to do something before I exploded.

Finally, his hot mouth closed around the peak, and I moaned, my hips rising toward him. He sucked hard and kissed over to the other one, taking it between his lips. I thought I would come from that alone. The pleasure was astonishing.

I knew if he wasn't going to last very long, then I would have to be close to climaxing before penetration. I took his hand and slid it between my legs.

"Show me how to touch you," he whispered. "I want to do it right."

I demonstrated how to rub up and down in long, slow strokes the entire length of my slippery folds. I felt the beginnings of an orgasm. Switching, I brought his finger to my clit and light touched myself with his hand. I let go, and he circled with exactly the right pressure. I guess he was a quick study. Soon, I was going to come, and I pushed his hand away. I made him sit up with his back against the rocky cliff and his legs out.

"You're ready, but I'm not," he said, and I looked down and realized he was still soft. But he was a young man and horny, so I knew I could take care of that. I gave him a look filled with lust and leaned down over him. With one hand, I lifted him and took him into my mouth.

"Oh, fuck," he said, and his legs tensed.

I brought my hand under his balls, playing with them while I sucked on him. His breathing became erratic, and when I glanced up, his eyes were closed in concentration. It only took a couple of seconds before he became hard in my mouth.

Shit, he was big. When he was erect, I could only take about two-thirds of him into my lips. I was hot for him, and I loved sucking him, but if I continued he would come too soon. I regretfully let him go and straddled his legs.

"Oh, Soph…" He caught my lips again, kissing me until I forgot everything except how much I wanted him inside me. I moved until his tip was lined up with my entrance, and I held his shoulders. Our eyes were locked as he slid about an inch into my wetness. It had been a long time since I'd fucked anyone and I felt tight.

I let him push in another inch and gasped as he began to spread me. Neither of us closed our eyes, unable to look away as he penetrated into my core. Soon he was halfway in, and I felt full. I pressed down farther and couldn't believe how my body was accommodating his size.

Unable to wait any longer, I dropped down the last few inches, gasping as he stretched me completely and our bodies connected. I rested my forehead against his, loving the feeling of him filling me. I pulled him tight against me, and we clung to each other.

My desire forced me to move. I began lifting myself and dropping down again. He was big. I felt every inch of him inside me, exciting all the nerve endings and rubbing against my G-spot. I felt my climax rising and moved faster.

Khellen was in the perfect position to suck my breasts, and he took one aching nipple into his mouth, sending pleasure straight to my sex. It was what I needed. I arched my back, offering my breasts to him as I continued to grind against him, building the pressure inside me.

He nipped at my breast, shooting me over the edge into ecstasy. I cried out and felt my body convulse, pleasure flooding every cell, as a mind-blowing orgasm blasted through my body. I continued to ride him, needing to feel it harder, faster, deeper.

My body started contracting, and I wrapped my arms around him, holding tight as the convulsions rocked me over and over. Finally, I rested my head on his shoulder, completely spent, my bones feeling like rubber by the bliss he gave me.

Without warning, he flipped our bodies, being careful to keep us coupled together. Now I was on my back, and he was on top of me. He pressed me into the moss, thrusting slowly in and out, and I breathed deeply as he stimulated raw nerve endings again. He held my gaze as he drove into me with a steady rhythm that gradually became faster and harder. My nipples rubbed against his chest, and I could feel his wiry hair between his legs rubbing against my clit and increasing my desire again.

I felt exposed as his eyes burned into me just like the way his body felt hot against mine. The fire spread and a second orgasm hit me. A few more thrusts and Khellen stiffened with a groan. His whole body tensed as his seed filled me. My contractions pulled at him, drawing everything out of him. And it felt right.

We lay there for a long time, with him inside me. I didn't want him ever to pull out, and when he finally did, I made a sound of despair as we separated. He kissed me gently, bringing me back to the pool and cleaning me. He held me for a long time on the stairs in the cool water. When my head was on his chest, I could hear his heartbeat. I felt a longing for him and wished his heart was beating for me. Still, he had worshiped my body, and that was almost as good.

At last, we put our bathing suits on and sauntered back to the little house, without saying a word to each other. We didn't want to break the spell.

Back inside, we stripped off our wet bathing suits and curled up in the bed together. Khellen wrapped his arm around me, his chest pressing tightly against my back, keeping me safe. I could have cried if it hadn't all been wrong. I wished I could keep him as safe as I felt right now.

I was so exhausted that I fell immediately asleep wishing every night could be like this one.

* * *

KHELLEN

I woke up with an acute awareness of my morning erection. With a start, I realized we were still spooning, and I had somehow wedged myself between Sophie's soft thighs with my hand cupping her breast. I even needed her in my subconscious. I dropped my hand between her legs and touched her until she became wet, making her body start twitching. Without planning it, I pushed into her a few inches. I couldn't help myself. She was so fucking tight that I might pass out from pleasure. I thrust in even farther, and I heard her gasp and become fully awake. Her butt pressed back toward me as I drove forward again and sheathed myself to the hilt. My pelvis was flush with her sweet ass, and she started to pant.

I moved slowly in and out of her hot, wet body. When I had imagined sex, I had thought it would be good, of course, but this was beyond what I had ever imagined. I lightly touched her clit the way she showed me. I felt Sophie's orgasm shake her body almost instantly. The feeling of her muscles gripping me was overwhelming, and I came inside her. Holding her hips against me as I pressed into her core, I emptied myself, filling her up. It felt like this was the way things were supposed to be.

She was breathing hard, her chest heaving as she recovered from her climax. I marveled at her beauty and perfection. Was it possible for her to ever be mine? Too tired to move, I lay inside her and drifted off to sleep again. Since she didn't pull away, I assumed she didn't mind. I liked being inside her. I loved feeling her surrounding me, and I didn't want to leave.

* * *

When I awoke for good later in the day, Sophie had left already. I felt an acute sense of loss and my eyes popped open. But I saw her coming out of the bathroom wearing a long, light green dress that made her look gorgeous and desirable. I felt like a beast had awoken inside of me, and I couldn't get enough of her body. Two times wasn't enough. Even if I could take her three times a day until I died, I wouldn't be satiated.

My heart jumped when she looked up and met my eyes. Her cheeks turned a rosy pink as she thought about what we had done last night and this morning. If only she were happy and not embarrassed. If only she had done it because she loved me. If only we could be more than friends with benefits.

"Khellen," Sophie said, perching on the edge of the couch. "Last night was amazing."

I nodded, sensing a "but" coming.

"But it can't happen again once we get back to your mother's house. I think this island has some seductive magic. But you know our relationship is too complicated already. Sex will make it even worse."

"No, it won't." I didn't want to agree with her and was already feeling the sense of loss.

"Look, it's not like I didn't enjoy it. I want you to know it was the most incredible experience of my life." Her voice dropped to a whisper. "It just can't happen again."

"Okay. I understood you the first time. You don't need to rub it in." I swallowed hard and turned away. She was right, of course. It was too complicated because she didn't love me the way I loved her and throwing sex in the mix had only made a difficult situation worse. My emotions were suffocating me.

I grabbed some clothes from my bag and headed for the bathroom, hoping she wouldn't see the conflict in my heart. When I passed through the door, I rubbed my eyes and stared at myself in the mirror. "She doesn't love you, Khellen," I told my reflection. "Get over it. There are other women. You can find someone else. Sophie isn't that special."

But I was lying to myself. Sophie was the one for me. And she was special because there was no one else that I could imagine myself loving. Things felt topsy-turvy. Now I was married to her, and we would have to live with each other for at least a year until she abandoned me and returned to Earth. The idea of celibacy was not exactly what I thought of when I imagined wedded bliss.

I put on my clothes and came out. Sophie was already packed and looked small and dejected from her position on the couch. She was curled up and hugged her knees to her chest.

"We can go back now. My mom said she was able to enter the information."

"Great." Sophie's eyes were lifeless as she stared at the pattern on the couch.

"Let's do it, then," I said and headed for the door. Part of me wondered why she felt bad. But I was so wrapped up in my pain that I couldn't spare any thoughts for hers.

"Fine," she said, getting up and striding past me. She looked furious, and my shaky emotions flared with anger in a direct reflection of her. What right did she have to be mad at me? I was the one who should be mad at her.

"We'll take a different way back," I told her, biting off an angry response. "Just in case."

"Whatever you want, husband." She fell in behind me as I took a detour onto another path that led to a second lookout point.

I winced at the sarcasm she placed onto her last word. The tension between us was enormous, and I couldn't believe I had pitied her a few minutes earlier. I had lost control of my emotions and knew I felt anger at how she had ruined my life by showing up randomly, enchanting me with her beauty, intelligence, and fiery red hair.

I stomped up the path until we arrived at the lookout. It was more sheltered than the first one, with purple bushes on all sides and a full, high stone altar from our ancient religion. The altar, which had once been a site for sacrifices, now served as a bench for visitors. The area was secluded because of the overgrown bushes. No one would be able to spot us if we rested here before arriving at the shore and swimming back home.

"We'll rest here," I said.

"Of course, husband. You make the rules." Her eyes were full of venom.

"You agreed to marry me. No one forced you, Sophie."

"No, of course not. I chose to marry you — out of concern, Khellen. I didn't realize that would make you my lord and master."

"What do you mean? You don't have to listen to anything I say if you don't want to."

"You never asked me if I thought it was a good time to go. We never discussed anything. You said, 'Let's go.' And away we went. Now you're telling me I have to rest. What if I'm not tired? You didn't ask me. I may have married you, Khellen, but I'm not your property or someone you can order around."

I grabbed her arm to make her stop. "I didn't mean it that way, Sophie. You know I'm not like that."

"I don't know anything about you, Khellen. I only met you face-to-face a few days ago." Her voice was getting louder. "And now I've broken my vow and gotten married. I fucked you. I've thrown my life away for you, and you treat me like I'm your servant."

"How can you say that?" I was practically shouting now, but I was too upset by her accusations to care. "I asked you to marry me, and you agreed. Nobody forced you to do anything. It was you who started things last night, not me."

"Now this is my fault?"

"It's nobody's fault! I don't regret a second of it. If I had a choice, I'd do it again. Right here, right now." I felt myself getting hard at the thought.

"Oh, would you?" she said, stepping up to me and getting in my face. "Take your wife and fuck her wherever you want to? Because you're the man of the house?"

"That's right," I snapped back, knowing it was a stupid thing to say. She was going to slap me. I was breathing quickly and so was she, her chest rising and falling with erratic breaths. That's when I noticed how hard her nipples were under the thin fabric of the sun dress. It shocked me. Was she as turned on as I was?

"You're saying you would fuck me right here if you could? Out in the open?" She was baiting me, but I thought I detected a spark of desire in her eyes, too. She wanted me to do it.

"Yes." I wondered where this was going.

"Do it, then, husband. You know you want to."

CHAPTER 11

KHELLEN

Had Sophie just given me permission to fuck her right here? The plants secluded the ledge from view, and this was supposed to be a private island, so there was no chance of anyone seeing us. Those were my rational thoughts. The other part of my mind imagined the idea of making love to her in a public place and made me aroused immediately. I searched her face and saw a hint of the anger she professed toward me, but it was fading quickly. Underneath was a new look showing naked longing and desire.

"It won't be gentle," I warned her, and her eyes got round. "Or slow."

"You talk like you have a lot of experience." If she was trying to upset me, it wasn't working. It only increased my lust. "Show me what you've got. Or are you all talk?"

I pulled at her dress and yanked it down so that her breasts spilled out. She gasped. I grabbed one and squeezed, pinching the nipple firmly, which made her moan. While I massaged one breast, I took the other in my mouth, sucking it.

Eventually, I pulled away and undid my pants. Her eyes were on my crotch as my pants dropped around my ankles, and she looked shocked when she saw the change.

"You're a different color than before." She was referring to my butt and groin, which had changed color after we had fucked last night.

"That's because I'm a fully mature Biyahan male after our evening together. One who is about to fuck you hard, Mrs. Lynch."

She took two steps back, eyes wide, and bumped into the altar. I looked at the altar again and realized it would be perfect for what I had in mind. I picked her up and set her on the platform, which happened to be at the height of my hips. I raised her dress up around her waist and pulled her panties down and away from her body. I felt the dampness of her juices. I was glad she was ready because I didn't want to wait any longer. If she wanted it, she was going to get it.

"Spread your legs, Sophie."

She opened them slightly, but it wasn't enough for me.

"Spread them wide. Your husband wants to fuck you." I took her knees and moved them far apart, then looked at her. Her body was beautiful to me. I brought my eyes up to hers and found her staring at me. "Tell me you want me to fuck you, Sophie," I said leaning forward and whispering in her ear, making her hips twitch. "I won't do it unless you say you want it."

She made an impatient sound, and I stroked her clit in tiny circles until she started to moan. Still, she wouldn't speak. I stepped back as if to leave.

"Stop," she said, putting her hand on my arm. She spread her legs even wider, face red. "I want you to fuck me."

The moment the words were out of her mouth, I had myself lined up at her pussy. I shoved in until I penetrated all the way inside.

"Oh, fuck," she said, her eyes rolling back in her head with pleasure. "Go slowly, Khellen."

I pulled out and drove into her again, fucking her in long, slow strokes that drove both of us wild. She was writhing and making a lot of noise, so I kissed her to keep her quiet. I sped up and pounded into her, exploding inside her as I felt her climax pulse around me. I kissed her as she came, swallowing her cries, which would have carried far across the lake if I hadn't done anything.

I pulled out as soon as the contractions from her orgasm stopped. I started to put on my pants while she tucked her breasts back into her dress and looked around for her panties. They had disappeared, vanishing off the cliff when I threw them away. The thought of her naked under that dress almost made me hard again.

Sophie's emotions had shifted again. "Is this how it's going to be?" she asked, her body and expression loose and relaxed from her orgasm. Then her eyes got angry. "You tell me when and where we're going to fuck?"

I stared her down, wondering if she was angry with herself or with me. "I was about to ask you the same thing." I held her face between my hands and kissed her deeply until I had to pull back or start all over.

"It's just a marriage of convenience," she said, adjusting the skirt of her dress with sharp movements. "I'm yours to use, both for saving your ass from dying and for fucking. I only want things to be clear. I mean, you want me to be explicit about everything, right?"

I gazed at my enigma of a wife in consternation. Then I shook my head and looked at the ground. Our first argument as a couple was resolved, I supposed. We had fought and made up all in ten unbelievable minutes. And now it seemed we were fighting again.

A marriage of convenience? I wasn't sure if it was convenient or not.

* * *

SOPHIE

I was frustrated with myself. Ten minutes ago I told Khellen that we couldn't be intimate any longer. How did I find myself begging him to fuck me? What was the matter with me? I felt like everything around me was spiraling out of control, and I didn't know how to get things back to the way they were supposed to be.

Falling in love with Khellen had made me crazy, and I was doing things that were totally out of character. It felt like I wasn't myself. And yet, in another way, I felt more myself than I had ever been before. It was baffling. When I turned to look at him, he had a small smile playing on his lips, which made me even angrier. I hadn't wanted to get married, but there he was, ordering me around. And I let him fuck me wherever he wanted to. I had broken my vows. We hadn't used protection, and it was all his fault.

My mindset lasted until we reached the shore. We were at a different spot, a little bit down from his house, not across from it. After entering the water to swim back, I started to calm down. I admitted to myself that I had freely chosen to get married, knowing full well what the consequences might be. I also realized I had enjoyed making love as much as he had, and I had asked for it up there on the ledge.

I swam away, thankful for the life band. I was exhausted, and the sleepless night had not recharged me at all.

"Are you doing okay, Sophie?" Khellen treaded water next to me, keeping himself up so effortlessly that it made me wish I could swim like him. I didn't want to admit that I was running out of energy, but I couldn't hide it. I nodded, avoiding his eyes.

"Give me your hand," he murmured. I relented and held out my hand, which he took and pulled me into his body. He wrapped one arm around my chest and under my arm. "Lie back and relax," he said, leaning back into the water and starting to kick with his feet. "I'll pull you."

I couldn't deny that I loved being in his arms. It was a pleasurable connection, and I once again rued the fact that I had fallen in love with him. I wondered if it would be enough to enjoy our friends-with-benefits arrangement.

The evening was surprisingly uneventful. We returned to the house where Khellen's mother filled us in on what happened while we were on the island. The government men had appeared, and the servants had tried to dismiss them. They had insisted on searching the house but, finding nothing, they reluctantly departed, promising to return the next day.

Khellen's mother had entered the marriage data and checked the system to see who was responsible for his arrest. She made sure Khellen's name was removed from the lists and innocently continued her regular daily activities. As the day progressed, no one questioned her. Eventually, she relaxed, put it behind her, and went about her business.

I felt a tremendous sense of relief, and Khellen did as well. We shared a smile, glad that he was safe. His mother didn't miss the glance we exchanged, but I didn't care. Khellen was not going to disappear. Maybe he didn't love me and never would, but I would get to spend the next year with him before I returned to my life on Earth.

I still had a strong drive to achieve and move up through the ranks of Single for Life, but I was also pushed in a different direction toward my incredibly handsome, sexy husband. Khellen didn't appear to want a long-term relationship with me, so that made my choice easier. At the end of the year, our time together would come to an end. As long as we kept it a secret, I could go back to my life on Earth.

"Morda's coming over," Khellen's mother said as we sat at the table finishing dinner.

"Why would she do that?" Khellen's fork stopped midway to his mouth.

"She thinks she lost a bracelet at the party and wants to look for it." She seemed unperturbed. "Is something wrong?"

"I guess not," Khellen said. "It might be awkward to see her again this soon."

His mother shrugged. "Help her find her trinket and send her off."

Turning to me, he asked, "Are you going to have a shower before bed, Sophie? Do you want me to get us a snack?"

My lips twitched, resisting the urge to smile. He was thoughtful all of a sudden. "Sure."

"Come down after you're in your pajamas, and I'll get it ready. I can shower later."

I thought I caught a satisfied look on his mother's face and wondered if she was changing her mind about me?

* * *

When I came back down, I found Khellen and Morda together in the living room. The sight of her made me filled with jealousy, though I don't know why. Khellen had never even liked the girl.

I stopped in the doorway, watching Khellen hanging over the back of the couch, searching for Morda's missing bracelet. His sweatpants had ridden down his ass. It wasn't enough to show his butt, but there was a definite red line above the waistband. Morda's eyes got big; she had apparently seen the same thing. She glanced at me, her look reproving and shocked. I became tense, not sure what she might do with the information.

Khellen popped back up holding the shiny bracelet in his hand. "I found it." He proudly held it out to her.

Morda plastered on a smile. "Thanks so much," she said, reaching for her jewelry.

"I was making a snack for Sophie and me. Did you want to stay for a little while?" He was almost maddeningly polite.

"It would be rude of me to refuse, wouldn't it?"

"Make yourself comfortable. I'll be right back." He vanished, leaving me alone with Morda.

She approached me immediately. "You little Earth bitch." She was practically vibrating with rage. "How dare you? He was supposed to be mine. Have you convinced him to sleep with you? Only sluts sleep with men outside of marriage, you know."

"What are you talking about?" No one had ever attacked me like that before.

"I saw that he's red down there now. He wasn't when I left. You fucked him, didn't you."

It was not a question, but an accusation. "I'm not answering that. It's none of your business what I did or didn't do."

She ignored me and went on with her tirade. "I was feeling sorry for myself for losing Khellen. But now I'm glad because he couldn't use me for my body." She wrinkled her nose at me in disgust. "You know he's not going to keep you, right? Once men get their way with you, they move on. He has to get married. His family isn't going to let him marry some Earth trash. Especially used goods like you."

I suddenly understood why women slapped other women. I didn't slap her, but I wanted to. I avoided her eyes, taking deep breaths, trying to control my outrage. As I did so, I rubbed my right hand on my left arm and caught the bit of compound again that felt like dried skin. I wanted to pull on it, but I knew that it might remove the covering and then part of the marriage certificate would be visible. That was the last thing I wanted to reveal right now. I rubbed my finger over it compulsively as I tried to calm myself.

She shook her head. "Did you think he might fall in love with you? Is that why you did it?"

I didn't say anything, but she read the truth in my eyes.

"You'll both regret taking what is mine."

What was she talking about now?

"Here we go," Khellen said, coming through the door. "Snacks."

He set the tray on the table and looked back and forth between Morda and me, sensing the tension.

"I just received a message, and I have to go. Thanks for finding my bracelet, Khellen," Morda said with an insincere smile. As she turned her back to him, she glared at me before leaving the room. We were silent until the front door closed, listening for any outbursts.

"Were you ladies playing nicely together?"

"Not really," I said, shaking my head. "She isn't as calm about losing you as we might have hoped."

"What did she say to you exactly?"

"Not much." I didn't want to relive the conversation in my mind. "She was very unpleasant. I don't want to talk about it."

"I think you should tell me. She always seemed like a troublemaker. I don't want to make you uncomfortable, but what if it's important? She could put us in danger, you know?"

There was no resisting the man. "First of all, she saw you were red."

"This isn't starting out well."

"She also said I was a whore and a slut because I seduced you and took your virtue."

He tipped his head back and forth as if admitting the veracity of that statement. "Well, she's right there."

"Khellen!" I swatted him, and he grinned.

"Sorry, but it's true. I was helpless before your beauty, Sophie."

I took a deep breath. "This is no time for joking," I said, trying and failing to be mad at him.

"I wasn't joking, Soph."

"You wanted me to tell you something embarrassing, and now you're not even listening to me."

"You're right. I'm sorry, Sophie. Please continue." He composed his face into the semblance of a serious expression.

"She said that she saw the maturation marking and wanted to know if I had slept with you. Of course, I told her it was none of her business." I decided to omit the part where she said Khellen would never keep me and that I was a fool for sleeping with him, thinking that would make him fall in love with me. I didn't see the need to share my deepest fears with him. But the other things came out in a rush.

"She thought your family wouldn't let me marry you because I wasn't good enough for you." Well, that was the one thing that was probably true. His mother would never have agreed if she thought there was another way to keep Khellen safe. "And she said I would regret taking you from her. She said both of us would regret it."

"What a drama queen," he said, shaking his head. "I wish Mother had never introduced us. What a disaster."

"What do you mean?" I asked. "Do you think she's going to do something?"

"I have no idea. She's determined, though. I would be surprised if she didn't try something." He flipped his arm over and started idly tapping the concealed certificate. "I'll see if I can talk to her. Maybe I can smooth things over."

"Please don't let anyone find out we're married, Khellen." I could see my world starting to crumble around me, and I began to panic. If I didn't have my career, I had nothing. It would take years to climbing the ladder again in another organization. I didn't want to start over. If Khellen didn't love me, I needed my work more than ever.

"Nobody's going to discover anything, Sophie. Don't worry. I'll talk to her and sort this out."

But she refused to talk him. He tried calling Morda. He even went to her house and her parents' house, but no one could find her.

"This isn't good," he said.

"Maybe she decided to visit a friend's house."

"Perhaps. I'm probably paranoid," he said, laughing a bit. I saw that the laughter didn't reach his eyes.

I went to sleep that night in a lonely bed. I was sure Khellen wouldn't have refused me if I had knocked on his door. I might have longed for him with every fiber of my being, but I couldn't make myself go and beg him to hold me. I had more self-respect than that.

It took me a long time to fall asleep by myself, but eventually I did. In the morning, I took a long, hot shower and put on my clothes. I went looking for Khellen downstairs, but he wasn't there. I went back upstairs and knocked on his door. No one answered me. I opened the door and looked around the empty room. After that, I looked in every room in the house, then shook my head for being silly.

I activated my virtual assistant. "Teri, where is Khellen?"

She put on a thinking face as if she were considering the question. I knew she was accessing the house and trying to locate him. "He's not in the house, Sophie."

I smacked my forehead as I realized that he had probably left to take a swim in the lake. I wandered down to the beach, enjoying the beauty of the purple trees. When I arrived at the shore, I put my hand over my eyes to shade them from the sun and looked around. I couldn't see him anywhere.

Fear struck my gut, and my breath started coming quicker. I ran back to the house and checked it over again. It was still empty. I grabbed my jacket and went to the front door. I yanked it open, but before I could burst out, I saw Fiona, poised to turn the handle.

"Fiona," I gasped. "I can't find Khellen anywhere."

"I know. He's not here." Her shoulders sagged. "The government discovered most of the things we did. I'm under investigation. They're holding him at the local jail." She looked at me furiously. "I hope you remember that is all because of you."

CHAPTER 12

SOPHIE

"I want to see him," I told Fiona angrily.

She gave me a scathing glance. "Why would you want to do that? You've made a bad situation worse. Now Khellen's life is in danger. You've done enough, don't you think?"

"Please, Fiona," I said, putting my hand on her arm. "I want to see that he's okay."

"Trust me. He'll be all right until he disappears." Tears welled in her eyes and she pressed her lips together. She paused briefly to compose herself before stepping over the threshold into the house.

"If you won't help me, I'll go by myself."

She spoke without looking at me. "They won't let you in."

I took her by the arms and turned her to face me. "They will if you come with me," I said. "Please."

She looked annoyed but soon relented. "I'll take you one time, but that's it. I have to figure out a way to get him out of there."

We made our way to the local jail. The wind was blowing softly through the indigo leaves, and I couldn't help smelling the lovely scent of flowers on the breeze. The air at home was full of smoke and pollution, the air of a dying planet. Why hadn't I said I would marry him without any conditions attached? I could have stayed here forever in this paradise. As Fiona and I walked down the path through the purple forest, we were silent until a question occurred to me.

"How did they find out?" I wondered. "I thought everything had gone well."

"It did. Someone tipped them off."

"Why would anyone do that?" There was a sinking feeling in my stomach.

"Does it matter?" I heard resignation and anger in her voice. "Someone told them the marriage records were forgeries. They saw the times didn't match. The informant suggested I faked the records to save my son."

"It was Morda."

Fiona continued as if she hadn't heard me. Wrapped up in her story as she was, maybe she hadn't. "What's ironic is that he's legally and properly married. But they arrested him because he's protecting you." She stopped walking abruptly. "Are you guessing it was Morda?"

"Yes. She saw something had changed." I didn't know how to tell her about the marking without revealing I had taken her son's virginity.

For once, she took pity on me. "She saw his maturation marking, I suppose. You're his wife, Sophie. There's no

151

need to be ashamed." For the first time, her expression towards me softened, and I saw the kindness Khellen had mentioned. "Sometimes things can't be helped. Don't feel bad. You've done nothing wrong. If Morda is responsible for this, she's to blame, that vengeful child."

"But how do we protect him if he's in their custody now?" I wiped my eyes and tried to pull myself together.

"I don't know, Sophie." She looked into my eyes. The despair I saw there disheartened me even more.

* * *

KHELLEN

When the force field came down, and I could see everything around me again, I thought my nightmare was over. I hoped I was only moments away from freedom.

But when I saw a guard escorting Sophie and my mother to the catwalk leading to my platform, my heart dropped. The expression on their faces told me they had no good news. They were coming to say goodbye. That's when the fear hit me. The thing I had worried about and tried so hard to avoid had finally happened, and I was powerless to stop it.

The two women I loved most in the world walked tentatively across the narrow walkway to my platform, clutching the railing tightly. I didn't blame them. Beyond the railing was an endless drop into absolute blackness. The environment was designed to discourage escape attempts.

The huge cylindrical room making up this block of the jail had hundreds of cells, each with the same slim catwalk extending at intervals around each level and all the way up. The platform cells were located in the middle of the huge stack.

When the force field disengaged, I sat on a round platform surrounded by a railing. When the force field was engaged, I was in a white room with a bed, a toilet, and nothing else. I couldn't see out, and no one could see in. The time I spent in there already made me a little stir-crazy. I needed to get out.

Sophie came across first. She gave me a tight smile but didn't touch me, which made me feel even worse. My mother pulled me into a hug, and I saw that she had tears in her eyes. "Khellen, are you all right?"

I nodded. "Am I stuck in here?"

"I don't know. Sophie thinks Morda was behind this."

I glanced over at Sophie, and she nodded.

"That's what she meant when she said we would regret it," I said.

Sophie looked bleak and avoided my eyes as she glanced around at the white balls at the ends of catwalks that looked they went up into the sky.

"I'm going to tell them." My mother made an announcement, glaring at Sophie, daring her to disagree. "We have to tell them you're married now."

153

"No, Mom, please. I don't want you to. There must be another way." Sophie didn't say anything.

"Guard," Mom called. "Bring the Warden."

A guard came across and seemed about to chew her out until she flashed a government access card indicating her rank. After that, he followed her orders.

The man spoke like an older person but must have had several rejuvenation treatments. He looked barely a day over forty. He looked annoyed as he came across the catwalk.

"What's this about, Fiona? It sounds like an open-and-shut case to me. He's not married. He's twenty-five. That means he's broken the law, and we are within our rights to arrest him and deal out the typical punishment."

"But he is married," Mom insisted. "Look, Warden, this is what happened. He and Sophie got married." She nodded at Sophie, who didn't say anything. "But Sophie has a job where it would look bad if she became married."

The Warden interrupted her. "This is getting pretty complicated. What kind of company wouldn't want you to get married?" He directed this at Sophie, but Mom answered for her.

"It's a long story," my mother said. "I'll tell you over lunch sometime. Just believe me. She didn't want anyone to know they were married. I agreed without raising a ruckus."

"You acted illegally, Fiona. Maybe you shouldn't be telling me this."

"I don't care, Seamus. Listen. No one would have been the wiser if Morda hadn't come to start trouble. They are married, Seamus."

"Give me your arm, Khellen."

I held out my left arm with the computer facing up.

"We concealed it," Mom said. "We couldn't have the certificate showing if we wanted to keep the wedding quiet."

The Warden called the guard over and spoke quietly to him. A few minutes later, the guard returned with a handheld device that he gave to the Warden before retreating across the catwalk.

"Hold it out," he said. He ran the scanner over my arm. "There's no information here, Fiona. Don't waste my time."

I saw that we had lost all credibility in his eyes.

"Seamus, I'm telling the truth. Don't you believe me?" My mother's voice was pleading now, and she wrung her hands together.

"I'd believe you if there were some proof. A marriage without a certificate is no marriage at all."

"Sophie can prove it. She can go to the doctor and have her covering removed. When she comes back and shows you, you'll have to let him go. They were married before he turned twenty-five. We have the proof. We just need a little time."

Seamus stared at my mother with compassion. "No one wants to lose a child, Fiona, I understand that. But there's the little matter of the law. If she comes back with a marriage certificate, we'll release him."

"Thank you," my mother said. "Come on Sophie. I'll take you to the doctor right now."

Sophie didn't say anything, but the look on her face was enough. Whatever remained of my heart was crushed. I knew she wasn't going to follow through. If she did, everyone would know that not only was I married, she was also married. Her supervisor would discover her secret and she would lose everything she had worked for on Earth.

As I gazed at Sophie, something changed inside of me. I had only been concerned for myself up until that point, but all I cared about was her safety when I was gone. I wanted her to have something for her when she returned home. I needed to let her know it was okay for her to do what she had to do. I wouldn't blame her for it.

I went to my mother, giving her a hug and a kiss. "I love you, Mom. Everything will be okay. Don't worry, all right?"

She looked puzzled. "Of course it's going to be okay. We'll be back in a few hours with the proof." My mother studied me with trepidation in her eyes. Did she know what was going to happen? I turned to the Warden. "Can we have a minute alone, please?"

The Warden nodded. He understood I needed to say good-bye. My mother still clung to the hope of my freedom, but I knew I wasn't going anywhere. They filed off the platform. I walked over to where Sophie stood, arms crossed, looking guilty and apologetic. The force field materialized around us, and we were alone in a white bubble.

"Khellen," she said immediately. "I can't do this."

"I know," I said, putting a finger on her lips. "I know." I held her gaze, willing her to understand. "I want your life to be intact when you go back to Earth. You didn't change your ticket yet, did you?"

"No, I didn't have a chance."

I shook my head. Unable to refrain from touching her one the last time, I wrapped my arms around her. She uncrossed her arms, linking them behind my neck.

"Don't say anything. Just listen. I want you to know I don't blame you. You tried to help me, and it doesn't matter what's going to happen now. You've been a good friend, Sophie."

"But Khellen—"

"No. I want you to listen to me, Sophie. Go to the spaceport, get on that shuttle, and go home. Tell your boss whatever you like, but start your new job." I kissed her gently on the forehead. "You're going to be single for life and save Earth from overpopulation. And you're going to know I'm behind you every step of the way."

She studied my eyes with sorrow etched in every line of her face. "I can't let you do this."

"You have to, Sophie. I have to."

"Why?" she whispered, tears shining in her eyes.

"I'll tell you the next time we meet." There wasn't going to be a next time. "I promise."

She kissed me then, and I responded, filled with a longing and sadness I couldn't hide. I held her tightly, burying my face in her shoulder.

"I love you," I whispered under my breath into her sweet skin.

"What?" she asked, searching my face. "I didn't hear what you said."

"You should leave. You have to pack your bags. It will be tough explaining everything to my mother, but do your best. It's okay if she doesn't understand."

I pressed the call button, and the force field disappeared. Sophie didn't move. I gave her a gentle nudge towards the catwalk. She finally reluctantly walked away. When she got to the other side, she lifted a hand and blew me a kiss.

I smiled and blew her a kiss back.

When the force field came up again, I knew she was lost to me forever.

* * *

An hour later, the force field powered down again, and the Warden beckoned me to come across. When I stepped off the catwalk, he put two thin bands on my wrists that immobilized my hands.

"Come with me," he said.

"Are you moving me?" My throat tightened painfully.

"In a sense." He guided me out of the cell block.

"Is this it? Am I disappearing?"

He looked back at me, shaking his head in disapproval as we quick marched down the hall. "The law's not difficult to follow. I don't know why we have trouble with you people. Still, you'll help build our population whether you get married or not."

"How's that again?" The Warden was leading me through a maze of corridors, and I had lost track of where we were.

"You're in good shape and have an excellent sperm count, according to our tests. You're going to a breeding facility."

I felt sick to my stomach. When the Warden reached a door at the end of the long hall, he moved his arm over the sensor pad. The door slid open, revealing a docking garage filled with hovercraft.

Seamus continued across the garage to a ship waiting on a departure platform. "The government needs the population to grow. If people don't follow the Edict of Marriage and start reproducing voluntarily, we enforce it another way." He glanced back as we reached the craft. "You didn't think they killed people of child-bearing age considering our population problem, did you?" It didn't make much sense when he put it that way. "You have your choice of natural reproduction or in vitro. Either way, your sperm is going to make babies. If I were in your place, I'd choose natural. There are lots of cute girls there who didn't follow the law, just like you."

"Why are you taking me there? You must have other people who can do this."

He turned to answer me as the door to the hovercraft slid open. "Your mother's a friend of mine. She made me promise to watch out for you until she returned with proof exonerating you. This is my way of fulfilling that promise."

"You know that's not what she meant."

"No, it's not. But it's all I can do considering the circumstances."

"This will break her heart."

"I know. You're a bastard for letting this happen." He motioned for me to get in the hovercraft before him. He climbed into the seat facing me and the door closed.

"You don't believe her, do you?" I stared at my restrained hands as the hovercraft slowly flew out of the garage. There wasn't anything visible between the bands on my wrists, but when I tried to pull them apart, they were solidly linked as if there were chains between them. The restraints were projecting force fields.

"It doesn't matter what I believe. The only thing that matters is the law. A marriage without a certificate is not a marriage."

"We have certificates, and we covered them."

"With what?" His voice dripped with skepticism. "There's nothing that could hide them from my scanners."

"Are you sure about that?" I said, holding his eyes.

"Yes." He added uncertainly, "What did you supposedly use?"

I rattled off the scientific name of the compound that I remembered from the bottle.

"Where the hell did she get that?"

I answered honestly. "I don't know."

He examined my arm again. I thought I might have convinced him, but then he shook his head. "No. You guys are trying to put one over on me. I'm sorry kid, but it won't work. Even with your magic compound, the device would have picked it up."

"What happens if Sophie comes back with a marriage certificate on her arm?" I was trying to find a faint ray of hope.

"The President doesn't want word getting out that we've gone soft. He ordered you moved three days early. We don't want anyone else trying this kind of hoax again. It doesn't look good for us."

"What about my mom? Is she going to be charged?"

The Warden shifted his eyes away from me. "The charges have been dropped. Your mother didn't commit a crime. She was trying to save her only son."

"You got them to drop the charges, didn't you?" His body language said it all. "You have feelings for my mother."

"And so what if I did?" His face looked defensive as he met my eyes.

"I thought you were just friends. But I'm glad to know someone will be looking out for her when I'm gone."

He looked contrite and a little bit guilty. "I'll watch out for your mother, boy. You needn't worry yourself about that."

I nodded. "Good."

He turned away from me and made himself busy with his comm unit, effectively ending the conversation.

The ride to the breeding facility took a few hours. I soon lost track of time and fell asleep in my seat. Finally, the hovercraft came to a stop, and the door opened. The landing platform was vacant. I could see a uniformed man crossing the facility. The Warden ordered me to get out.

"This is it, then? I'm stuck here no matter what?"

"No one comes back after a disappearance, Khellen." His artificially youthful face held genuine compassion. "I'm sorry."

The hovercraft door closed, and I watched it fly away. Behind me, a guard poked my back.

"Let's go, stud." He didn't bother to contain his amusement at my situation. "This is your life now. Welcome to the disappeared."

CHAPTER 13

SOPHIE

The scene with Fiona went as horribly as I imagined, even after I explained Khellen knew it didn't matter if we came back with proof of our marriage. She refused to believe me, trying to convince me to visit the doctor using every argument she could imagine. In the end, she threw me out of her house, cursing me and slamming the door in tears.

I didn't blame her.

I picked up my bag and followed Khellen's instructions. I went to the spaceport to wait for my flight. It wasn't departing until the next day, but I knew sleep was impossible. Instead, I wandered through the shops trying not to think of or remember anything.

It was a long night, and by the time morning came around, I was bleary-eyed and sick to my stomach from lack of sleep. I went to the bathroom, feeling nauseous. A minute later, I was puking in the toilet. Something felt wrong.

I took out my BioScan and set it on the floor, standing over it in the bathroom stall. It scanned me and beeped, letting me know it was done. At the same time, the alarm rang for boarding the spaceship. I picked up the BioScan and placed it in my bag, planning to check the information on my computer later.

At the waiting area, I pulled out my computer, checking my health statistics and looking for the reason I felt sick. I hoped I hadn't caught an obscure alien disease. I looked at the illness section, but nothing came up. I checked a few other pieces of information I thought might hold the explanation, but couldn't find anything.

That was unusual. The BioScan was the best health device on the market, and I paid a lot of money for it. I hoped it wasn't failing when I needed it the most.

I tapped my foot nervously, impatient for the flight to begin. I was ready to get off this planet and get away from here. I wanted to forget everything and press the reset button on my life.

I decided I must have missed something in the report. I went back to the beginning and started checking everything again, looking for any markers indicating abnormalities. When I got to the fertility information, I didn't skip it this time but went through every line just as I had in the other sections.

And that was when I discovered the problem. In a sense, I had caught an alien disease.

I looked around and wondered if people could tell by looking at me. Of course not. No one would see anything for another three or four months.

Apparently, I was fifty-six hours pregnant.

* * *

The automated announcement system called my flight, but I didn't move. I thought about those last moments with Khellen, replaying them in my mind, slowly coming to the realization that Khellen loved me. That's why he sent me home. He thought he was doing what was best for me and giving me what I wanted. I had been so blind convinced that he cared nothing for me, but the signs had been everywhere all along.

I put my hand on my belly. We had made a child together. I couldn't get on a flight and abandon him to his fate, no matter what we said before. I had to go to the doctor and get the compound removed. When I showed them my certificate, they would have to let him go. I would have to figure out what to do about Single for Life later. I grabbed my bag and ran for the door.

I jumped into a self-driving car outside and programmed it for the address of the doctor's office. I had saved it on my computer. Next, I sent Fiona a message, telling her I was going to have the compound removed.

I was sitting impatiently in the waiting room when I got an emergency message from Fiona. I picked up, walking down the hall for some privacy. "I hope nothing's the matter," I said.

"Don't worry about the certificate right now, Sophie. Can you come down to the jail? I'm afraid something's wrong. They won't let me see him."

"I'll be right there," I promised, already walking out of the building. Had they made him disappear already?

Fiona and I waited at the compound for three hours, going through miles of red tape until someone finally gave us permission to see the Warden. I wondered if they had delayed us on purpose.

He addressed us as soon as we sat in his office. "You need to give up. I know he's your son, but he can't expect the law to adjust for a single person. The law bends for no one, especially the Edict of Marriage. You know that."

"Seamus…" — she was crying openly now — "He's my only son. He's all I have left of Harry."

Instead of relenting, Fiona stalked over to his desk and pressed against it. She leaned in and glared at him. "Give me the number."

"What good will that do you? They never come back."

"It gives me peace of mind," she said. "If it doesn't matter, why not tell me."

After a moment of thought, the Warden relented. "It's 241. That's all I can do for you, and it's more than I should." We turned to leave immediately. "One more thing, Fiona?" he called out. She turned back, her eyes filled with hope. "Are we on for lunch next week?"

Fiona laughed a little manically. "I don't know if I'll ever be able to have lunch with you again, Seamus. I can't even think about it right now."

"You know I'm only doing my job."

"I'll think about it," she said gently, but I believed she cared for this man, and the feelings were mutual. That explained why he had helped us so much. I doubted he was this lenient with most people. He didn't seem like the type.

We left the office and walked down the hall, side by side, not saying a word. A moment later, we heard the Warden's voice behind us again.

"Fiona." She kept walking, but he caught up with us. He called her name again, but she continued to ignore him. He shook his head, exasperated. "I have something for you."

He took her hand, and she moved to pull it away before she realized he had placed something in her palm and was wrapping her hand around it.

"It's a present," I heard him whisper in her ear. "Please forgive me."

She studied his face and blushed. "I'll think about it." She gave him a peck on the cheek and walked away with her head held high.

When we returned to Fiona's house, she took me into her bedroom.

"It's safe to talk in here. I wouldn't let them install any security equipment in my room. They're detaining Khellen in Holding Center 241. This will get you access to the building." She held up an access chip the Warden had hidden in her hand. "Once you're in, you'll have to blend in and find him. I don't know how, but the two of you will have to get out somehow."

"How am I involved this much?" I asked, flabbergasted. I just married him. I'm not a secret agent!

"The Warden is helping us, but I believe he had to conceal his actions in case someone was watching. With his information and security chip, you should have clearance to enter the building."

I raised my eyebrows.

"He wants me to be his girlfriend, but I'm a bit old for that sort of nonsense." The light in her eyes belied her words.

I examined her for a long moment, thinking about what I had lost. "If he loves you, you shouldn't waste it. It could all go away in an instant, and then you'll want it back." My loss rushed over me in a black wave.

Her face was filled with compassion. "You're probably right, Sophie." She paused and added, "And I want to apologize to you. I thought you were toying with him. I didn't know you cared about him. I thought you were going to break his heart."

I couldn't look at her. "You might be right about that last one."

"He will forgive you. He loves you, Sophie. That's why he sent you away. We all make mistakes. It's what we do about them that makes us different."

169

I paced back and forth across the room. Khellen was gone, and I was his only hope of coming back from being disappeared. That was almost worse than having no hope at all. I was an average girl without any special skills. What was I going to do?

"The journey will take all day. Then you can wait until nighttime to enter the building. Maybe you can locate him while everyone else is sleeping."

"I'm not sure I can do this, Fiona. Do you have any other information that might help me?"

She sighed. "No one has ever come back from being disappeared."

"This is hopeless." Tears filled my eyes. "Why did you even bother getting the number and this access chip?"

"Khellen will be the first to come back. And you're going to be the one to get him out." She looked intently at me, and I could tell she thought I could do it.

I had no idea how I would accomplish the task. Where would I find the courage for something this monumental? All I knew was that if Khellen disappeared, I might as well, too. Was there a better way to go out than trying to save your true love?

"I'll do my best."

* * *

The hovercraft trip felt like it took forever, even if it was only a few hours. I told the pilot to set me down after we had come as close as reasonably possible to Khellen's location. He didn't know about the holding center because it was a secret facility hidden underground.

I had programmed the coordinates of Holding Center 241 into my computer. I would have to trudge along the route on foot, taking the path to the building that provided the most cover.

I tried not to think of the baby inside me and the fact that my husband was a prisoner of the state, possibly in a breeding facility that was off the official record. Unfortunately, that just gave me more time to think about the fact that I was the only one who could free him. It was a lot of pressure. I needed to come through for Khellen, for me, and for our baby.

Up until this point, my life had been comfortable. I wasn't a hero, but I was prepared to act like one.

* * *

The door into the facility was carefully concealed, but I was able to locate it using the precise coordinates. Darkness was only a few minutes away. I swiped the access unit over the door's control pad, and it unlocked and slid open.

That was one obstacle down.

I covered my face, making sure my appearance was obscured on any cameras and slipped through the door

171

before it closed again. Once in the building, I had an alternate method of determining Khellen's precise location. The particular wedding bands Khellen purchased had tracking chips in case of an emergency. It seemed like an extravagant add-on, but now that I needed it, I was glad it was there.

Fiona had activated Khellen's locator, letting me find him in the facility. I looked at my screen and studied the building schematic. The flashing green dot indicated Khellen was ten floors below me, all the way at the bottom. I wondered why he was down there, and I hoped to get that information once I found him.

I activated my virtual assistant and asked if Teri could tell me who was awake and on guard in the building. She quickly discovered it was confidential information. Teri didn't have access. I had her download information from the Warden's device and she smiled, telling me everything I wanted to know.

"Is there a way into the basement from here?"

Teri began to iterate all the possible ways to descend.

"Limit yourself to ways no one will discover me. I have to stay hidden, Teri," I whispered.

"They don't use the cargo elevators at this time of day, but the elevators only go down to the ninth floor. There are conduits large enough for cleaning robots. If you took the cargo elevator down to the ninth floor, you could crawl through the ducts down to the basement."

"What's the purpose of the tenth floor, Teri?"

"Oh, that's easy," she said. "Solitary confinement. With visitors, of course."

"What do you mean?" I strode quickly towards the cargo elevator, which Teri said was only used once a week when supplies arrived. "Solitary confinement means there are no visitors."

"Solitary has a different meaning here. Breeding is the only purpose of the prisoners."

"But—"

"Inmates are subjected to solitary confinement when they refuse to breed. They're kept there until they start to give in, which doesn't take long. An inmate of the opposite sex is installed in their cell. It's someone they've previously shown interest in, but it doesn't matter who it is. The second inmate is in a state of high sexual arousal. You can imagine what usually happens."

"They mate?" I guessed, getting into the elevator and pressing the button for the ninth floor.

"They mate wildly and for hours. It has the side effect of removing any remaining reservations to taking part in the breeding program."

Less than a minute later, the elevator opened silently, and I walked out onto the ninth floor. Teri directed me to the conduits, and I used the Warden's chip to access the maintenance panels. I climbed in and began crawling along. I wasn't sure about the correct direction, but I decided as long as I kept heading down I would end up at the right place. Soon, I came to a ladder. I tried not to look down; the shaft seemed to have no bottom at all.

I gripped the ladder tightly and descended carefully, taking my time. Eventually, I crawled out of the conduit onto the tenth floor. The level was quiet and dark. It seemed abandoned. I turned Teri's volume down to a whisper and crept out into the hallway. She gave me directions, and while there wasn't anyone around, there were probably cameras everywhere. I asked Teri to mask my appearance so that even if the cameras captured my image, it would be blurry.

"This is the room you're looking for," Teri whispered.

I stood outside the door and listened. From within came the unmistakable sounds of people having sex. I felt my cheeks go warm. I hadn't thought about what I would find when I got there. What if Khellen had been forced to have sex with other women while he was there? I hadn't left him with a reason to save himself for me.

Why was I hesitating? Had I gone there to get him out or not? It didn't matter what he had done. I had to get him out. I waved the device at the door, and there was a click as it unlocked and slid open. I was hesitant to go in, not sure of what I would find. But I gathered my courage and stepped into the cell.

It smelled of dirty aliens and sex.

The room was pitch black, and I could only see using the light that came from the hall. There was a man with his back to me in the corner with a naked woman wrapped around him. She was straddling him and rhythmically bouncing up and down, making keening sounds. She was facing me, and I saw the pleasure on her face as they fucked.

"Khellen?" I hoped it wasn't him. That's when she came, screaming, and the man dumped her unceremoniously off him and onto the floor. "Khellen?" I said again, afraid.

When he turned around, all my worst fears were realized. He looked terrible, with red, bloodshot eyes. I wondered if he had slept since he arrived. He seemed skinnier, though it seemed impossible. The haunted look in his eyes disturbed me the most.

"What are you doing here?"

"I came to get you." My voice sounded small in the nasty little cell.

"You can go right back out. I don't want you to get me. As you can see, I'm busy here."

He gestured to the woman, who was lying curled up on the floor in a post-orgasmic daze, coughing as if she were going to lose a lung. Was something the matter with her?

"Khellen, I won't leave you here."

"You misunderstand me, Mrs. Lynch. Allow me to be clearer." He walked over to me, and I could smell the other woman's juices on him. "Get out." He put his hands on my shoulders and pushed as hard as he could, sending me flying into the hallway, where I landed on my butt. He shut the door, leaving me on the floor with a sore ass, a confused heart, and no way of getting back in. I had dropped the access chip inside his cell.

CHAPTER 14

KHELLEN

I sat in the darkness of solitary confinement with my back against the wall, waiting for anything to happen. Once again, I wished for my computer unit, which guards confiscated as soon as I arrived. The disappeared didn't get electronic devices.

My feeling of noble self-sacrifice had lasted all the way until I arrived at the holding center and understood what my life had become. Then I became furious thinking about everything I had lost. I was angry at the government and myself, my mother and Morda, but most of all I was furious with Sophie. It was because of her I was here. The rational part of my brain knew I was incorrect, but I couldn't reason myself out of my rage — not in this cesspool they called a government facility.

There was something about this place that corrupted my mind. Every ounce of love had turned into a white-hot burning hatred. How could anyone be as selfish as she had been? How could she have sent me to this place? I should never have told her to walk away and leave me in the cell to rot while she went home to a happy life.

Holding Center 241 was a facility where those who refused to procreate naturally, by getting married and having children, were forced into breeding for the good of Biyaha. On the first day, my guard took pity on me and had given me information and tips for surviving. The Warden had made it sound like I would be dating in here.

It was not remotely like dating.

We were allowed to select our partners as long as we had sex at least three times a day with three different people. No protection was used, of course, and some of the inmates had sexually transmitted diseases. The infections that were rampant in the population didn't hurt the fetus or the fertility of the parents, so they weren't a concern to the government. Inmates saw a doctor once a month for treatment, but that wasn't frequent enough, and the medications rarely helped. The government wasn't even pretending to try and stop the spread of the diseases.

When the guard told me about the STDs, I made a plan. I would refuse to cooperate, and then I would escape, somehow. I guess it wasn't a plan. It was more like a fantasy or a dream. But it was all I had, and I was sticking to it.

I learned how they used solitary confinement as punishment. After a stay in solitary, the inmate was usually released back into the main population with their will broken. There was a rumor that they put something in the food to encourage mating. It was the most disgusting place I had ever heard of, and I had to get out.

Even worse were the other communicable diseases that could be contracted from the air or from touching a person. A pulmonary disease had killed three people while I had been there. They were trying to contain it, but they were struggling with all the bodily contact between inmates. Before I went to solitary, there had been discussions of quarantine, but they hadn't taken any concrete steps. If they lost more breeders, they would have to do something about it. A reduction in the population would be counterproductive.

What struck me as interesting was that the people who died from the lung disease had all been off-worlders. The Biyahans got sick and coughed a lot, but off-worlders were dead within a few days of contracting it. I couldn't help but think about Sophie. As angry as I was with her, I was relieved at the same time that she wasn't anywhere near this hellhole. Right now she was on a nice clean shuttle, heading back to Earth. Maybe she was already back home in her cute apartment. I pictured her bedroom, where she'd recorded most of her hologram messages. Thoughts of Sophie didn't belong in this horrible place.

From the start, I had refused to have sex, so they put me into solitary almost immediately. I didn't know how long I was there because it was dark and I had no visitors. My only companion was a bucket in the corner for me to shit and piss in. I couldn't mark the passage of time. Still, I knew they would put some desperate woman in here with me sooner or later, and I had to be ready. I wasn't going to have sex with a random person. I felt like I was losing my mind, though, and I hoped I wouldn't do anything stupid.

When they transported people to the solitary confinement level, there was usually only one guard. More guards escorted punished inmates because they were more likely to struggle. While I was in the general population, I saw two prisoners taken away. My plan was to attack the guard when he brought in my potential mate. After I overcame the guard, I would take the cargo elevator to the main level. There wasn't tight security. Most people, no matter how much they hated this place, were so disheartened they had no will to escape.

Eventually, the door opened. I heard the scraping and jumped up, legs stiff and body sore, but adrenaline pumping through my body.

The guard shoved the woman into my cell, and she fell to the floor coughing. They had sent me one of the sick ones, of course. It didn't matter to me. I was taking the opportunity to get out of here right now. I ran at the guard, taking my chances, not thinking, only attacking. I tackled him and managed to get in a few punches on his head. I was wild, and all I wanted was to get away. When he lay still, I raced down the hallway as fast as I could, looking for the elevators. I tried to remember the path I took when they moved me here.

A moment later, my whole body stopped moving, and I fell to the ground in agony. I looked up to see the guard standing over me. He grabbed my arm and dragged me back down the hall, making no effort to be gentle. The stun was wearing off by the time he got me back to the cell, and I started to yell.

"No! I won't go back in there!" I could scream, but my body was still immobilized.

"Yes, you will. You'll stay there until you stop making a scene and go fuck that woman."

"How can you do this? You people are monsters!"

He stared back at me, probably used to madmen shrieking at him. "Stop fighting and make things easy for yourself," he said, dropping me onto the floor in the blackness and shutting the door.

As soon as I could move, I sat up, went to the corner, and tried unsuccessfully to think of something else. Anything other than this awful place. My mind filled with pain from the electric jolt. There was nothing but the pain and the sound of coughing.

I hoped she wouldn't infect me. In theory, the coughing would probably only make me sick. It killed the off-worlders.

I felt the woman's body wrap around my back. "I need it badly," she said.

"You're going to have to wait." I pushed her away, making her crash onto the floor again. She coughed for a long time. As soon as she caught her breath, she was back, thrusting her hips at me. Her hands reached around, trying to undo my pants.

I couldn't push her away forever. I was afraid to sleep because she would try to have sex with me when I was helpless. And I knew my body would respond. The woman was insatiable and seemed more desperate than me.

Finally, I thought of a way to get her to leave me alone. I could give her what she wanted.

When she came at me the next time, I grabbed her and pulled her into my lap. She wrapped her legs around me, moaning, and I felt that she was naked already. I dropped my hand down and found her clit. She gasped and began thrusting her hips at me while I touched her.

I sat down on the floor while she was on my lap. She bounced up and down against my hand as I stimulated her, making a high-pitched wailing that grated on my nerves. It was potentially the least sexy thing I could imagine. A noise cut through my haze of pain and my focus on getting her to leave me alone. It was the door opening again. Why was the guard back already?

Then I heard something I thought I'd never hear again. Sophie's voice.

"Khellen?"

At that moment, the woman came, screaming, and I pushed her off my lap, getting to my feet, filled with anger and fear for Sophie's health.

"Khellen?" she called again, sounding as if she hoped it wasn't me.

I moved stiffly towards her, the pain from the stun still throbbing in my limbs. I knew I must look terrible. I hadn't eaten or slept much since I arrived. "What are you doing here?" I asked, glaring at her as terror filled me. The woman was coughing again like she would never stop.

"I came to get you," she replied timidly. I suppose she hadn't expected this reaction from me. There was something about this place that was getting to me and making my personality unrecognizable. But what was stronger than my need to escape was my desire to protect Sophie. If she caught the lung disease, she might die. "Well, you can go right back out. I don't want you to get me. And as you can see, I'm busy." I pointed to the woman spasmodically coughing on the floor. If she had come this far to rescue me, she wouldn't leave without a good reason. Thinking that I didn't care about her was the best way to keep her safe right now.

"Khellen, I won't leave you here."

My heart clenched. Even after everything she saw, she still wanted to help me leave. "You misunderstand me, Mrs. Lynch, allow me to be clearer." I moved towards her, trying not to stumble on legs still weak from the stun. "Get out."

I grabbed her shoulders and pushed as hard as I could. She landed roughly in the hallway, and I shut the door before she could get up and come in again. I only hoped it had been in time. No one was sure how the disease spread. It could be an airborne virus or from skin-to-skin contact.

The woman on the floor had stopped coughing and was lying quietly. I hoped she was sleeping. My legs gave out, and I sat down in a heap. I hoped the stun hadn't done any permanent damage to my nervous system. I noticed something glowing on the floor as I sat down, and I reached out to pick it up. It must be Sophie's. It looked like a security device. How had she gotten it? It explained how she penetrated so far into the compound.

I felt horrible. My body was racked with pain and I needed sleep badly. My emotions were in turmoil from seeing Sophie again. My overriding concern, however, was getting Sophie out of there before she contracted a fatal cough. What should I do?

Since Sophie had gotten in, she knew how to get out. We had her electronics. But what if I inadvertently infected her? Last time I had sent her away, she had gone without a backward glance. Perhaps she had done the same thing this time.

"I'm still here, Khellen." Her whisper was audible through the barrier.

I didn't understand why she hadn't run away when I rejected her. She had gone quickly enough the first time. Why was she staying now? If we managed to get out of here alive, I hoped there would be adequate time to figure out Sophie's motives.

"I'm not leaving you," came her voice.

I ignored her, trying to decide the best action plan. I didn't have much time before the guard came to check on me.

Then I had an idea. If Sophie's electronic device was a multipurpose tool, it might have a scanner. A scanner set to the highest level might kill any virus or bacteria. It would give us both a chance to get out of here alive and together. I got slowly to my feet and opened the door with the device.

Sophie didn't say anything but stood looking at me silently. I handed her the piece of electronics. "We have to do one thing before we can leave. I'll scan you first."

She picked up the device and inspected it carefully. "You have it set to the most powerful level. Do you think it's safe?"

"There's a contagious disease spreading through the facility. Off-worlders have been dying from it, and the woman in there is showing symptoms. We need to decontaminate ourselves, or you might catch it."

Her eyes got round, but she didn't argue with me.

After we had scanned each other, she led us at a frantic pace in a different direction. We heard someone coming and hid in a closet until the footsteps passed by us. We continued down the corridor that ended at the cargo elevator. She used the access override to unlock it, and in less than a minute we were at ground level. When the door opened up, we crept out. We hadn't gone five steps before we heard a shout behind us.

"What are you doing there?"

"Run!" Sophie said, grabbing my hand and dragging me behind her. We made our way to the loading dock, stopping at an open bay door. Two workers were off-loading supplies from the cargo hovercraft floating outside.

"Where are you going!" the female worker shouted. "Stop! You're not supposed to be here!" She ran towards us, pointing a blaster in our direction. We dropped to the floor, crouching behind some pallets of medical supplies.

When the worker edged around the pallet, Sophie grabbed the woman's arm — the one holding the blaster — and twisted it. She pulled the woman down and hit her. Sophie grabbed a piece of twine from the debris on the floor and flipped the woman on her stomach, quickly tying her hands behind her.

I gave Sophie a surprised look. "We have to do whatever it takes to get out of here," she said.

The male worker had held back during all the action, and I saw that he didn't have a weapon.

"He doesn't have a weapon," I whispered. "Let's make a break for it."

We took off, heading straight for the large bay door. The man tried to stop us, but I punched him in the stomach and pushed him out of our way. As if suddenly remembering something, he raised his arm and pointed something at the door. It started to rumble shut.

"Come on, Khellen." Sophie was yanking my hand, but my stiff body couldn't move as fast as it needed to. The door dropped quickly - it was already a third of the way closed. "Khellen, you have to run faster!" Her tugging on my arm made it ache even more. I felt my body begin to shut down.

"This is all that's in me," I said.

"Find more!" She was screaming at me, and I wanted to run, but I felt a secondary paralysis from the stun, and I couldn't do anything about it.

The door was halfway down, and we were too far away. I stumbled and would have fallen if Sophie hadn't pulled me forward. We were almost there, but the door was nearly shut.

With Sophie helping me, maybe we could make it. After a few more feet we would be in the clear. When I was almost to freedom, my body seized and I fell to the floor, unable to bring my hands up and prevent my head from hitting the floor.

The last thing I remembered was my skull smashing into the stone.

CHAPTER 15

SOPHIE

A few feet from the bay door, Khellen collapsed to the floor as if he had lost control of his limbs. It looked like he lost consciousness when his head smashed into the ground. The door was almost closed, but I hadn't come this far to give up now.

I scrambled and slid under the door, reaching the other side while still holding onto Khellen. I don't know where I found the strength. I reached under his arms and pulled as hard as I could. Khellen came sliding out just as the door slammed closed behind us.

They would be coming after us. We needed to get away. But Khellen was unconscious and probably hurt. I eyed the cargo hovercraft. I could fly, but I had never piloted a vehicle this large before.

I was going to have to learn quickly.

I wasn't sure how I could get him into the ship. He was much heavier than me, and now his body was dead weight. I walked around the craft and found a floating lift used to move cargo into the building. It was designed so anyone could operate it with minimal training, so it didn't take long for me to figure out how to lower it, drag him onto the lift, and move him into the hovercraft.

After I had boarded the ship myself, I hustled to the control panel and pressed the button to close the door.

Then I studied the array of buttons, lights, and sliders. When I recognized the ignition controls, I reached out and managed to start the engines. Maneuvering carefully off the loading dock, I realized flying this ship wasn't much different from ships I'd piloted before, except for the size. I did crash into something, but it was small, and I hoped it was irrelevant. I took a deep breath, plotted a course, and got us moving.

When I checked the sensors, there was no one behind us. I headed away from Holding Center 241 and didn't look back.

* * *

After an hour moving at the highest speed I dared, I set the hovercraft to a more normal velocity and put it on autopilot. I called Khellen's mother on an encrypted channel.

"Fiona," I said, as soon as she answered. "I think we need to get off this planet as soon as possible. Do you think you can get us two tickets on the next ship out of here? It doesn't matter where we go."

"Sophie, what happened? Do you have him? Are you all right?" She looked flustered.

"We're both alive, but we're going right back to prison unless we fly out of here."

"I'll do what I have to do. I'll get them somehow and call you right back."

"Don't forget to encrypt the line."

She nodded and the screen went black.

I climbed over boxes and containers until I reached Khellen, who looked pale and was breathing shallowly. Was there anything I could do?

I tried to remember my first aid training but couldn't think of anything, and my training on humans might kill an alien. I thought there might be a first aid kit in the vehicle, so I combed through cabinets and compartments until I found one. I brought it back to Khellen and activated it. A male VR assistant's voice started telling me what to do.

"Please scan the patient." When I finished the scan, the computer gave me further instructions. "Use the decontamination unit to neutralize the pathological viruses."

I guess using a random piece of electronic equipment as a sterilization device wasn't a safe medical procedure. I poked through the kit for the decontamination unit and ran a full procedure on Khellen. Next, I attached the unit to the ceiling and cleaned myself twice.

Khellen had terrified me when he told me about the disease. It explained why he treated me roughly when I found him. The woman in his cell— I didn't want to think about him mating with her — had been coughing, and he wanted to protect me.

When I finished, the computer recommended decontaminating the vehicle as well. After another scan, it declared we were virus-free. I blew out my breath in relief.

"Use the coagulator to stop the bleeding at the site of the wound on the patient's head," the man's voice said.

I did as he instructed and made Khellen as comfortable as I could, getting him onto one of the floating stretchers instead of leaving him lying draped across crates. I covered him with a blanket and kissed him briefly on the forehead.

He might never forgive me for how I had betrayed him, but I had made partial amends by rescuing him. If I could safely get him to a place where the government couldn't reach him, I could live my life with a clear conscience.

I hoped he would forgive me, but I didn't expect him to. Especially after seeing the anger in his eyes when he pushed me out of his cell. I had left him to be taken to the prison and abandoned him because I was scared, all to further an ideal.

I straightened my shoulders and pulled myself together. This was not the time for a pity party. I picked at the compound, which had lifted more each day since Fiona applied it to the marriage certificate. The exposed bit of corner was now big enough to grab with my fingers. I pulled on it experimentally, feeling immediate pain with the glue-like substance tugging on the delicate skin of my forearm. I wasn't going to get it off this way.

191

I wished I had an opportunity for a doctor to remove it, but I doubted there would have been time for that and to free Khellen. There was no way to know for sure, and I might drive myself crazy with fruitless thoughts.

A tone signaled a communication from Fiona. "Sophie, I'm on an encrypted line, and I'm transmitting the tickets now. I've arranged for medical transport for Khellen directly to the shuttle."

"What about…"

She ignored me and continued with her monolog, answering my question before I got a chance to get it out. "Don't worry about the Warden's men. They won't bother you. If they ask you anything, give them the code included with the tickets. He's been kind enough to assist us."

Fiona had convinced the Warden to help us, no doubt. I briefly wondered what she had promised and if she would regret it. But I had no time now to ponder what favors Fiona had offered to save us. Besides, she had feelings for Seamus, so our situation may have given her an excuse to do what she wanted. I tore my thoughts away from Fiona's love life and focused on her instructions again.

"When you get to the spaceport, a medical transport team will meet you. They will bring Khellen to the shuttle and into a private cabin. Using this route will avoid any problems with him not having identification. They will have the required information to get him checked through. The documents say you will be allowed to stay with him in the private cabin because you are his wife. I suggest you remain there for the entire trip."

"Where are we going?" I asked. Anxiety was making my stomach feel tense. I rubbed it, and with a start remembered that I had a child growing inside me.

"The flight will take you to Shveitz. It's a neutral planet that takes in political refugees. Once you arrive, you're going to be on your own, Sophie."

I nodded at her. "Thank you, Fiona. We'll be in contact as soon as we can."

Fiona teared up. "Please take care of him."

"I will." Of all the promises I had given in the past month, this was the one I felt deep within my soul. I would take care of Khellen and bring him to a safe place, no matter the cost to me. If he decided to kick me out of his life, I could live with it. But until he was safe, I would protect him.

She said good-bye, and I cut the connection.

* * *

Everything went according to plan. The medical team met us and accepted Khellen as a patient. After checking Fiona's documents, they fast-tracked us onto the shuttle and into a room just for us. The technicians checked us over once we were inside. They didn't have to decontaminate us again. As part of their onboarding procedure, the physicians scanned us with their equipment and found nothing irregular.

They were slightly concerned with Khellen's head injury but determined he could travel as long as he had it checked when we arrived on Shveitz. They administered a tranquilizer to put him in a light coma for the duration of the trip. I slept most of the time and Khellen rested quietly under his sedation. His color and injury improved as his body healed.

The medical technicians said the coma would wear off about three hours before landing. When we got closer to the planet, I booked us a hotel in the central city and arranged for medical transport for Khellen, in case he had problems regaining consciousness.

I impatiently waited for Khellen to wake up as the lilac-colored planet came into sight on the cabin's view screen. I didn't know what would happen when he woke up, but I certainly wanted to get things moving. I was tired of waiting.

The planet got closer and closer, and he continued to sleep. I resigned myself to the fact that he wouldn't wake up, and we would need the medical transport after all. I strapped Khellen in before we landed, kissing him again as I fastened the straps on his bed. I secured my restraints and we landed without incident.

In the docking bay, a recorded voice welcomed us to the planet, instructed us to remove our belts and gather our belongings. I released myself, and as I reached for Khellen's straps, he finally opened his eyes. I helped him undo his restraints, and he sat up, looking around in confusion. He glanced down at his white hospital sweatpants and the long-sleeved shirt. There were frown lines between his eyebrows as he tried to orient himself.

"I have a lot to explain." I helped him get up and handed him his shoes. "The shuttle has landed, and we need to get off and go to the hotel. We can relax there, and I'll tell you everything."

"Where are we?" He fumbled with his shoes. He managed to get them on his feet, but his fingers didn't do the delicate work, so I had to tie them for him. His problems could be related to being shot or remnants of the induced coma. The technicians said he would recover quickly, but might have small motor issues for a while.

"We're on Shveitz," I told him, standing up. "Can you walk?"

He took a few hesitant steps. Even though he looked stiff and sore, he was able to move. "It seems like it."

"Good." I grabbed the backpack laden with a few things Fiona had sent. "Let's go."

We were fast-tracked through security again. I made a mental note to write Fiona a long thank-you letter.

When we exited into the spaceport, we were met by a jostling crowd of reporters and local police officers. One woman stepped forward and held her hand toward us, palm out. "Halt," she said. "You're under arrest."

195

I guess I wasn't going to get a chance to write that thank-you note.

* * *

KHELLEN

I had been groggy since regaining consciousness. Sometimes there was short-term memory loss after a medically induced coma. Bits and pieces of what had happened floated in and out of my mind, but I couldn't remember anything clearly. I obediently followed Sophie off the shuttle. I had to trust her for everything right now.

"Oh no," I heard Sophie say under her breath when she spotted the police officers.

"Halt," a female officer said. "You're under arrest."

Sophie drew herself up to her full height and faced the officer. "Why?" There was a steely defiance I hadn't heard before.

"We've been asked to detain you. The government of Biyaha has a warrant out for your arrest."

"That's why we're here," Sophie responded, her eyes intense. She was trying to remain calm. "We're seeking asylum from political persecution."

"On what grounds?" the police officer asked, not looking sympathetic at all.

"My husband was being held prisoner by the Biyaha government."

"Do you have evidence?"

"You want proof they were holding him? How could I prove that?" She was doing her best to hide her desperation.

"We're not looking for proof of his incarceration. If you can prove you're married, we have no reason to detain you. He has an outstanding arrest warrant for breaking the Edict of Marriage. If you can show evidence of your marriage, we will not honor the Biyahan request to hold you."

Sophie's worried look made no sense to me. If we were married, we would have proof; why was she so concerned? I looked down at my left forearm. There was nothing there. A memory danced around the corners of my mind but eluded me.

The police officer looked down at my forearm as well. "There's nothing here," she said pointedly.

"They're hidden underneath a chemical layer." Her excuse sounded ridiculous, even to me. "It has to be removed by a doctor under anesthesia."

The police officer rolled her eyes and shook her head.

"I'm telling the truth. You have to believe me." Sophie pleaded with the officer, who was moving towards her.

197

The reporters had been listening raptly, with recorders held over their heads. Suddenly, one of them spoke up. I wondered if they were broadcasting live to their news stations. "Is it true that this man is one of the disappeared?" His equipment indicated he was from Earth.

Sophie's head whipped around to see who had spoken. She noticed the Earth logo too and hesitated before addressing the question. "Yes, he is."

"You claim to be his wife?"

Sophie paused again, staring at the insignia on his jacket. "Are you transmitting live to Earth?"

He nodded.

She cut her eyes over to me, and it seemed she had to decide something painful. She slowly pressed her lips together and gave a tiny nod. "I am his wife," she said, and lifted her head, first staring directly into the camera and then looking back at the police officer. "If I can prove it, will you let us stay here and leave us alone?"

"Of course I will. That's what I said, isn't it? I'm not here for fun. Show me proof and you are free to go," the police officer replied. She looked annoyed but interested.

"Okay." Sophie took a deep breath. She swallowed and bit her lip, raising her left arm. Sophie had everyone's attention now, and she knew it. As she lifted her right hand towards her left arm, I saw that it was shaking. I wondered what she was going to do.

She grabbed hold of a small flap of dried skin protruding from her left forearm. With another deep breath, she pulled down sharply. She cried out in pain, and all at once, there was blood everywhere. Everyone gasped.

I didn't understand what that had to do with showing we were married.

I pulled off my shirt and moved to stop the bleeding, but she pushed my hands away. Turning her forearm to the crowd, she announced in a loud voice, "My name is Sophie Lynch, and I'm Khellen Lynch's wife."

Through the veil of blood, the marriage certificate and wedding band were visible to everyone — police, reporters, and Earth via a live feed.

She stepped up to the police officer, letting her arm drop down to her side. "We seek political asylum on Shveitz. Is that enough proof for you to let us in?" she asked, holding out her arm to the police officer.

The policewoman looked shocked, but she nodded curtly.

"Sophie, we need to clean you up." I was unable to focus on anything else. I took her arm and dabbed it with the white hospital shirt, ignoring the chilly air of the spaceport that was giving me goosebumps on my bare chest. I paused to run my fingers across the picture of us on the certificate. Seeing the picture made all of my memories come flooding back. "Sophie," I said, meeting her eyes.

She saw that I remembered everything. There was fear in her eyes, as I slowly wrapped my shirt around her arm trying to understand what she had done.

"You're free to go, Mr. and Mrs. Lynch," the police officer said, approaching us and speaking more courteously now. "Your records are clear. You are welcome on Shveitz for as long as you need to stay. No one will try to arrest you again." She nodded an apology at Sophie and addressed the reporters. "You got your story. Please vacate the area now. Mrs. Lynch needs medical attention." She raised her authoritative voice above the din of the excited reporters.

"There's a medical transport waiting for us outside," Sophie said, her face was worried and anxious as she gazed at me. She didn't seem to notice that her forearm wouldn't stop bleeding and was soaking the white shirt crimson.

"I don't know which one of us needs to use it more." The police officer kindly escorted us through the crowds of people catching flights. Everyone moved aside when they saw Sophie was bleeding, and soon we were speeding away in the medical transport hovercraft.

The doctors evaluated both of us and stopped the bleeding on Sophie's arm. They thought the bleeding looked worse than it was and wrapped her arm in a white gauze bandage before they dropped us off at the hotel. After reaching our room, we collapsed on the couch in silence. I didn't know where to start and neither did she.

I gently took her hand, making sure to touch the good arm, without the bandage.

"No, Khellen," she said before I could say anything. "Let me talk first."

I stopped, studying her face as she spoke.

"I want to apologize. I'm sorry for walking away and leaving you the way I did. It was selfish and cruel, and even if you didn't love me, I still should have helped out a friend. I shouldn't have listened to you when you told me to leave. I've been a coward, and I don't expect you to forgive me. I wanted to get that off my chest before I left." She stood up then, but I wouldn't release her hand.

"Sit down. I want to know why you came and rescued me from that place if you're as selfish and cruel as you say."

"I couldn't leave you there after I had realized I had done something wrong. It wouldn't be right to leave a friend in such a terrible situation."

"Even if I didn't love you, you should have helped out a friend. What does it matter to you whether I love you or not, Sophie?" My heart was beating quickly. She was staring down at our interlocked fingers but looked up as I asked my question. Our eyes locked on each other.

"Because," she whispered.

"Why?" I asked, so quietly I almost didn't hear myself.

LISA LACE

"Because I love you, and I want you to love me back."
Her eyes filled with tears. One rolled down her cheek,
and I watched it fall and make a small dark spot on her
pants. "Back in the jail when you didn't tell the Warden
that we were married, I thought you might feel the same
way, and that was why you hadn't revealed the truth. I
wondered if you wanted me to have the life I thought I
desired." She stumbled over her words and finally
stopped. "Do you think you can forgive me, Khellen?
Even if you can't love me?"

I shook my head. "No."

CHAPTER 16

SOPHIE

I held myself together. I was determined not to fall apart until I got outside the room. I had my whole life to cry. But he wouldn't stop talking.

"I won't forgive you, Sophie, because there's nothing to forgive."

Tears spilled down, and I was helpless to stop them. "I need to hear you say it. Please tell me you forgive me."

"I forgive you, then. But not because I think you did anything wrong. I'll do it because you asked me."

"Why?"

"I would do anything you asked of me." He brought our joined hands to his lips and kissed mine tenderly. "It doesn't even matter if you asked or not."

"Then I have another request," I said, brushing away tears with my other hand. "You promised to tell me why you sent me away earlier, Khellen."

He looked at me strangely. "Because I love you," he said directly. "I didn't want you to see me like that."

I didn't let him finish what he was saying. I wrapped myself around him in a hug so tight that I was afraid I might hurt him. He pulled away from me, giving himself enough space to put his lips on mine. Suddenly we were kissing like there was no tomorrow and like we hadn't seen each other in years. We were two people in love.

* * *

We had our clothes off in record time and fell on the bed, needing to be as close as we could, feeling like we had nearly been separated forever. Our bodies twisted together, kissing and touching as my excitement increased. He rolled me onto my back, and I spread my legs wide, feeling him at my entrance.

"I need you inside me, Khellen." I gripped his ass tightly. "Please."

He closed his eyes and leaned forward, pushing in slowly, maddeningly, inch by inch. "I," he said, pressing in deeper. "Love." He was filling me up with every word. "You, Sophie Lynch." As he said my name, he gave a quick, sharp thrust that drove him home completely. I gasped as I took him inside me.

He moved tenderly, plunging in and out of me as he held my gaze. "I love you, and I don't want you ever to doubt me again. Do you understand?"

I nodded, unable to speak. He rubbed against every nerve ending I had, and the pleasure was uncontrollable.

"Answer me." He leaned down and drew a nipple into his mouth. He swirled it with his tongue, sucked on it hard, and gave it a tiny nip.

"I understand," I moaned. "I love you, too, Khellen."

He drove into me, and every movement took me higher. I arched upward, my body answering him, our hips colliding in perfect rhythm.

"You're mine," he said, his pounding becoming faster and more frantic.

"Yes." I was beginning to pant.

"Say it."

"I'm yours."

"And you'll never be single again."

"Never," I got out.

"You'll never be barren because you're going to have my baby."

"Yes," I hissed, the wave building inside of me.

"Say it."

"I'm going to have your baby, Khellen." Sooner than he knew.

"And..."

My orgasm crested, overtaking me and I cried out, lost in the ecstasy. He found his release too as I clenched around him. Exploding in sensation, I shattered into a thousand pieces, writhing under him as he pressed me onto the bed, pinning me beneath his massive body. I trembled with pleasure until I was spent.

Eventually, we lay still.

"You may be mine, Sophie, but I'm yours, too. You own me, body and soul, and I don't want to live without you." He covered my face and neck with small kisses that made my hips come alive again. I smiled with my eyes closed.

"There's something that I need to tell you." I opened my eyes to look at him. "It's good news, I think."

He tilted his head curiously. "What is it?"

"I'm going to have your baby."

"I know." His eyes were warm and smiling.

"In about nine months." I kept a close watch on him for his reaction. "I'm pregnant, Khellen."

Suddenly he was kissing my breath away. "I can't believe it," he said, pulling out of me and then bringing me close to him again. I threw a leg across his hip. He put his leg between mine, moving closer until we were chest-to-chest. "We're going to be a family."

I nodded, thrilled and relieved that he was happy about it, too.

"Sophie, you promised you would tell me everything."

"That's true, I did." I made myself comfortable. "I didn't intend to fall in love with you, Khellen. I came here to make sure you got married and didn't disappear."

He laughed. "You can check that off."

I grinned. "You were so handsome and charming and sweet that I couldn't help myself. I fell for you. But when you asked me, as your friend, to protect you from the law by marrying you, I got the message. I thought you weren't interested in me."

"That was the wrong message. That night at the hover party, after we kissed on The Boat, it was all over for me."

"We were such idiots."

"That's in the past now," he said, kissing me.

"On the island, I knew you didn't love me, but I thought, 'If I could have this one night to remember for the rest of my life when I am alone and single back on Earth, I will be happy.'"

His grip on my back tightened. "That night was unbelievable," he said. "I was thinking the same thing."

"What happened right now was amazing, too." I burrowed my face into his neck. "Is it always going to be this good between us?"

"I hope so, Sophie. We have our whole lives to figure it out."

I closed my eyes. "When I couldn't find you the morning after we got back from the island, I thought I would lose my mind. I'm the biggest dope on the planet."

He kissed my forehead. "But you came for me."

"Your mother helped. She arranged everything."

"I know you don't get along very well."

"At the end, we weren't exactly friends, but we were allies, at least."

"I'm glad," he said. "I've never seen anything like what happened at the spaceport."

"I had no choice," I said, shaking my head. "They weren't going to let us stay. They were going to turn you over to those bastards on Biyaha again. I swore to your mother that I would take care of you." I stopped, taking a shivering breath. "Of all the vows I've made and broke in the last month, I swore I would keep that one, no matter what."

"I still can't believe you ripped off the covering." Awe and admiration were on his face. "I've never seen anything like it." He lifted his head, supporting it with his hand. "You should have seen the looks on those reporters' faces. That's when I knew you cared about me. Because once I thought everything through, I realized you knew the reporters were transmitting back to Earth. A juicy story like ours would be all over the news."

I nodded.

"You risked everything for me and thrown away any chance of returning to the life you left behind."

"I love you," I said, gazing intently into his eyes. "I'd do it all over again if I had to…but I hope I never have to do anything like that ever again."

"You won't if I have anything to say about it," he said.

I suddenly felt sleepy.

"Rest, love," he whispered into my ear. "You've earned it."

* * *

Khellen and I had been looking at houses on Shveitz. We needed a permanent place to stay before the baby was born. We sat in a café, discussing the different locations we had seen over a bite to eat.

"I think the house on the acreage makes the most sense," he said. "There'll be room for the baby to play."

"I liked the apartment at the top of the other building."

"But there's no yard," he pointed out.

"You're right. And I did adore the bathroom in the house on the acreage, too."

"There's a nice big tub in there," he said, lifting one eyebrow. "Big enough for two."

I tried to look prim, but my attempt fell apart when he grinned at me. The idea of a tub big enough for two was a plus. "Did you hear from your mother yet?" I asked, changing the subject.

"She sent a message when you were talking to the real estate agent," he said. "I forgot to tell you."

"What did she say?"

Khellen's mother had been communicating with us every day after we let her know we were safe and expected a child. She was considering taking an early retirement so she could move to Shveitz to help after the baby came. She wasn't going to stay permanently and was keeping her house on Biyaha. I thought the Warden had something to do with her decision since they were officially a couple now. She had forgiven him for his part in Khellen's disappearance. I hadn't, but I wished them well.

I wasn't sure how to feel about her coming to stay with us. I didn't want her trying to tell us how to raise the baby, but I knew we would need assistance.

"She's put in for retirement."

"Great." I don't think I succeeded in keeping the ambivalence out of my voice. The extra set of hands would be helpful. She was supposed to take care of the housework so I could focus on the baby, which sounded like a dream.

"She doesn't believe in what her department is doing any longer."

"I hope not," I said, finishing my drink.

"Did you ever get a response from Nora?" he asked.

I shook my head sadly. "No. She's angry with me for quitting and giving up on everything she believes. I tried to explain in my message that the vow didn't mean anything on Biyaha. There's no overpopulation problem where we're living now, but she doesn't understand."

"I'm sorry. I know how much you valued her friendship."

"You know, I still feel the need to do something about Earth's population problem."

"Why don't you start a rival organization? Even Singler for Life."

"Nothing like that. It's just the beginning of an idea. Maybe we can think it through when the baby's older. It doesn't have anything to do with me being single."

"As long as I get to stay married to you and you have my baby, that's all I care about."

"Really? That's all that matters?" I repeated.

"Well, maybe not everything." He grabbed my hand and pulled me up. "Let's go. We'll take the house with all the land." Khellen swept his new computer over the scanning tab in the middle of the table, paying for our meal. He glanced at my baby bump as it came into view. "You look lovely," he murmured into my ear as we moved to the door. "I can't wait to get you alone."

"Khellen," I said, blushing. "Someone might hear."

"Someone's going to hear you all right because you'll be screaming like before."

I shushed him but knew I was looking forward to it. So was Khellen.

CHAPTER 17

SOPHIE, ON EARTH

"A girl came in today, Khellen," I said, ruffling my hair in the mirror. I thought I still looked pretty good after having a baby. I hadn't lost my figure, and I had worked hard to lose the extra weight. I thought it made me intimidating, which was good for business.

"Doesn't that happen every day?" he called out from the kitchen of our tiny Earth cottage.

"She wasn't very pretty, and I told her. I think I was too honest. You know I don't usually care about superficial things, but she wasn't trying at all. She was getting on my nerves too."

"Yes, dear." I heard the clink of dishes. I hoped dinner was almost ready. I was starving.

"Are you even listening to me? She says, 'How do you know I want to apply? Especially after what you said about my appearance."

"Don't be too hard on those girls, Sophie." He came behind me and put his arms around me. I smiled, laying my head against his shoulder and reveling in the familiar feeling of safety and happiness. Khellen had found ways to keep in shape on Earth despite the lack of swimming, and his body was still amazing.

I refocused, coming back to the conversation. Maybe I was hard on the girls, but they had to be tough if they wanted to become mail-order brides for aliens. If they couldn't handle a rough interview, how would they survive a whole year on an alien planet in a foreign culture?

"I said something back to her." I adopted the haughty tone I used for TerraMates. "'How do I know you want to apply? Because you didn't walk out when I said you were ugly.'"

"I can't believe you, Sophie!" Khellen burst out laughing.

"I most certainly did. It was the truth. Anyone who wasn't already committed and had been offended by my comment would have walked out immediately."

"You're right. Still, I feel sorry for the girl. You don't need to be completely honest all the time," he said. "Come and eat."

He took my hand and led me to the table. "She kept her application open, I assume?"

"Of course. She'll need to be tough. She's going to a planet without technology."

Khellen nodded, dishing out the food. "I wonder how long Maria is going to sleep," he said, changing the subject.

"Let's enjoy it while it lasts," I said. I loved my daughter, but having a break once in a while felt fantastic.

Maria was the reason we had moved to Earth. Despite its problems, I loved my planet, and I wanted to raise my family on my home world. It didn't take long for me to convince Khellen. We needed to make money, and I rapidly formalized the business plan for TerraMates.

I still wanted to solve the overpopulation problem, but I would do it my way. I had gotten the idea from an off-hand comment Khellen once made about me being like a mail-order bride. That's what we did - we arranged marriages between women of Earth and alien men.

With all the franchises across the globe, we manage to send approximately a hundred thousand women off-planet every year. It doesn't sound like a lot, but every woman counts. Since we only have a low divorce rate at the end of the one-year marriage requirement, we were also helping couples find each other.

When we were ready to retire, we were thinking about returning to Biyaha. There was a new political movement starting there with a different platform than the existing government. The new party had made information about the breeding centers available to everyone, and the intergalactic reaction had been universal outrage. Biyaha was starting to think there were better ways to address their population problems, and had begun a new program catering to people from overpopulated planets. The ex-pat community on Biyaha was growing.

Khellen's mother had said we could have the cottage on the island whenever we wanted it. But that was a long time away, and I had lots of work to do with TerraMates before I was ready to retire.

"Our life on Earth is just about perfect," I said.

"Almost perfect. How long do you think Maria will stay asleep?" Khellen's hand had moved to my thigh.

I met his eye. "What were you thinking, Mr. Lynch?" I recognized a familiar tingling in my body.

"I thought we might have the house to ourselves for another hour." He leaned in to kiss me.

"And why would that please you?"

"Because I want to make love to you," he said. My breath caught in my throat. "I love you, Sophie."

"Still?" I said, losing myself in his eyes.

"Always."

If you enjoyed this book, please review it on Amazon! Your review helps me succeed as an author.

To stay up-to-date on my latest releases, sign up for my newsletter at:

http://lisalace.com/newsletter/

OTHER BOOKS BY LISA LACE

WATER WORLD WARRIOR: A TERRAMATES NOVEL

Why would I want to be married to an alien?

I should not have applied to TerraMates! The idea was crazy. I'm a young woman, in the prime of my life.

But I was desperate.

When I landed on another world, his appearance intrigued me. He dripped sexuality and moved like an animal. We have three days together before he sets sail without me. Am I going to escape or submit to my desires?

TAKEN: A TERRAMATES NOVEL

What happens when TerraMates runs out of applicants?

There's never a shortage of wealthy alien bachelors looking for the thrill of mating with a human. They want our women.

But despite the promise of riches, sometimes the pool of available brides runs dry.

How does TerraMates find more girls, and where do they go? When Lyzette gets taken off the street, she finds out.

WATER WORLD CONFIDENTIAL: A TERRAMATES NOVEL

He needed a wife. I wanted an alien lover.

The first time I saw Jori, I hated everything about him. He didn't care about anything except himself. On the other hand, his body was spectacular, and his muscles were firm. I couldn't stop thinking about him.

When TerraMates gave me the chance to marry Jori, I took it. I knew I needed the money. What I didn't know was that Jori's exterior was a facade, and he had kept secrets from everyone his entire life.

ALPHA'S ENSLAVED BRIDE: A TERRAMATES NOVEL

Knowing the future isn't a blessing. It's a curse. Especially when you've seen your death.

I'm going to die in the arms of someone I have never seen before. He's a person I will love, but I don't know anything about him.

When TerraMates matched me with Airik, I couldn't believe it. This sexy alien could see the future, just like me. I wasn't alone anymore. I quickly found out he knows nothing about Earth or humans. I married him, but will I be safe with him?

AUCTIONED TO THE ALPHA: A TERRAMATES NOVEL

The innovative TerraMates business has been a runaway success. Who wouldn't want to marry an alien?

Seeking to expand, TerraMates has opened new locations with different business models.

Eden is looking for a fresh start and is one of the first mail-order brides from New York City. As soon as she signs the paperwork and collects her credits, she blacks out.

When Eden wakes up, she's been married to an alien bounty hunter. She's ready for a new beginning, but all she knows about her alien husband is that he's handsome and dangerous. Eden never dreamed she'd be chasing criminals through space!

WRONG ALIEN: A TERRAMATES NOVEL

Life isn't worth living without an Internet connection. I'm always on the computer, video chatting, and even reading books on my phone.

It was natural for me to use the TerraMates app to find a husband.

I didn't know they would match me with a sexy alien who was afraid of high technology and send me to a mysterious planet where the penalty for having a smartphone was execution!

NAIMA: A TERRAMATES NOVEL

I never thought I'd find my soulmate through a mail-order bride agency. I never thought he'd be an alien warrior.

He calls me naima. His beloved.

When I'm on my way to meet him face-to-face, my shuttle is attacked, and we crash onto a planet in the middle of a war. I didn't sign up to be an alien comfort woman. I need my naima to rescue me.